Total-E-Bound Publishing books by Natalie Dae and Sam Crescent:

Shades of Grey
Rude Awakening
Forced Assassin

I0570384

By Natalie Dae:

Fantasies Explored:
Think Kink
Think Kinkier
Kinky Thinking

A Gentleman's Harlot
Lincoln's Woman
That Filthy Book
Shadow and Darkness

Collections:
Stiff Upper Lip: Minure Maid

Anthologies:
Bound to the Billionaire: Waiting for Him

By Sam Crescent:

The Valentines:
Robert
William

Love and Death:
Love, Death and Justice

Office Hours

FORCED ASSASSIN

NATALIE DAE
and
SAM CRESCENT

Forced Assassin
ISBN # 978-1-78184-538-7
©Copyright Natalie Dae and Sam Crescent 2012
Cover Art by Posh Gosh ©Copyright July 2012
Interior text design by Claire Siemaszkiewicz
Total-E-Bound Publishing

Published in 2012 by Total-E-Bound Publishing, Think Tank, Ruston Way, Lincoln, LN6 7FL, United Kingdom.

FORCED ASSASSIN

Dedication

It was a pleasure working with you, Natalie.
You're an amazing writer and I look forward to many
more projects like this.
—Sam

Prologue

Waterman settled more comfortably in his leather office chair. It squeaked until he found the right position. "Each woman will put the goods in the requested location. Each woman will receive ten grand for doing it. Each woman will live the rest of their lives thinking they got lucky. End of."

Kemp sat opposite, swivelling in his seat, one foot on the floor, the other resting on his knee. "What if they look in the bags? We won't know if they do."

Waterman sighed. Kemp got on his nerves when he acted like this. "If they look and we find out, then they're fucked, simple as that. We have all their addresses. We know which woman has what information. Anything leaks, it won't take a scientist to see who peeked."

"I still say it's a risk." Kemp pinched his beard-covered cleft chin.

Sunlight coming through the window behind Waterman made Kemp's black hair shine. Waterman wished he had a full head of hair like that, instead of his bald nut. Still, he had everything else he could possibly want—money, prestige, the ability to put the fear of God into almost everyone. What was a bit of hair loss compared with that?

"No risk," Waterman said. "They signed contracts not to open the bags. The people who want the goods think they'll get them—that's what they're paying us for. They know there's a risk of their misdemeanours being made public, but they think we'll do our best not to let that happen. Frankie let the women know, in that lovely way of his, what might happen to people who poke their nose where it isn't wanted."

"Jesus!" Kemp shook his head. "Any one of them could go to the police if he's used his usual threats."

"Nah. He did it in the right way. Said it but didn't, know what I mean? Got a way with words, that one. The lure of money means a lot to women like them. They're all skint, all need to pay off a few bills hanging over their heads. Bailiffs coming to the door—amazing what ten grand can stop. Worry, sleepless nights, all that. The chance to start again. That's why I picked them. They're desperate, living on edge all the time. My offer was like a gift from God."

"But still—"

Waterman leant forward, slapping his hands onto the desk. "Are you questioning me, fucker?"

Kemp sat upright, both feet planted on the floor. His face reddened, and he loosened his tie. "No. No, I just—"

"I just nothing, right? Those women were checked out. Thoroughly. I'd bet my old dear's pearls not one of them will look in those bags. Now, if you'd rather I call the whole thing off and send *you* to deliver the goods, you've only got to say the word."

Kemp snorted. "Fuck no."

Waterman chuckled. "Didn't think so. Don't like the idea of the government sniffing about and finding you, do you? Them knowing you know what's on those microchips?"

"No." Kemp closed his eyes and shuddered.

"As far as they're concerned, I don't even know what's on them, but, if I send you to deliver—because lately you keep querying every fucking thing I do—well, Frankie might let it slip you've looked on the chips, know what I'm saying? It's easy for them to get rid of you."

"Why are we even going through the charade of dropping the bags off when we're sending our own people to steal them back? We're not even keeping to our end of the deal. It would have been cheaper if you dropped them off, would save you paying the women. Why don't you do it?"

"Why have a dog and bark yourself?"

"I suppose…"

"We need to make it look like someone else entirely has taken the goods from their hiding places, not us. Those government agent fuckers are dangerous to mess with."

"I know, but—"

"There you go, then. Shut the fuck up."

Chapter One

Bishop. He rolled the word around in his mind, testing whether it fitted. He quite liked it as names went. It wasn't a bad one, better than some of the others he'd had, but it wouldn't be his long enough to matter, anyway.

They never were.

He stared across the hotel dining room—with white cloths draped over round tables big enough to seat six—to the woman sitting in the far right-hand corner. She hadn't clocked him watching her since yesterday—or at least he didn't think she had—and ate her Beef Wellington in delicate morsels, gaze fixed into the far distance as though she had a lot on her mind. And she would have, if the other marks were anything to go by.

He looked at his own plate, the food there unappealing, and wished he'd opted for the Wellington himself. A pork chop—undercooked, the fat around the edge soggy and unappetising—seemed to mock him, the mashed potatoes next to it just as sloppy, just as stomach-churning. He pushed his plate aside and reached for a glass of water, catching a glimpse of his reflection owing to the harsh lighting from the chandeliers.

Bishop sighed. He appeared in sore need of sleep, those dark circles beneath his eyes the bane of his life. The inch-long scar on his cheekbone from an assignment last year had at last faded from deep pink to a paler shade, but it still marred his otherwise handsome face, still reminded him he'd failed.

The one who got away...

He grimaced, placing his glass on the table, turning it this way and that for want of something to do. Occupying his mind on occasions like this was always difficult—he watched, he noted, he waited, over and over again, until his marks did what he'd been told they would and he had to finish them.

A lock of his black fringe caught on his eyelashes, and he shook his head. Focusing on the woman again, he wondered why she'd been chosen for the job. That long auburn hair of hers would get in the way if she didn't tie it up, and her slender figure brought forth thoughts of a ballerina rather than an athlete who could cope with running for her life if the need arose. It would, too, if things went to plan...and she'd be running from Bishop, lungs straining, leg muscles screaming.

That's if she ran. He might get lucky and catch her before she had a chance to flee, but things rarely worked out like that when he was on a job. He'd had to fight for the end result every time, Fate or Lady Luck poking her big nose in, stirring things up so he failed to get an easy ride...

He laughed. Couldn't remember the last time he'd ridden a woman. Relationships were few and far

11

between in his line of work. It was pointless trying to have one, his long hours, days away from home — weeks, sometimes — didn't bode well for keeping a woman happy. Still, he had his right hand, and that had been enough. Until he'd set eyes on Fallan Jones. Was that her real name or was she hiding, the same as him? He shouldn't care, hadn't in the past, but then his marks weren't usually so bloody…attractive.

Fallan. He rolled that name around too, liking it more every time it echoed in his mind. He imagined calling it out when he came, when she clutched him to her, legs clamped about his waist, crossed at the ankles, heels driving him deeper inside a cunt he imagined would be tight. Soaked.

His cock twitched — the last thing he needed if Fallan got up and left the dining room. He willed it not to grow fully erect, thankful when it didn't. He needn't have worried. It looked as though she was going for three courses tonight. A waiter whisked her plate away, and another came by with desserts on a trolley laden with sweet delights.

She ought to be on that trolley, sweet delight that she is.

No, he mustn't think of her like that. She was a mark, nothing more, someone who needed taking out before she did any more damage.

She pointed to a high mound of profiteroles, and the waiter spooned several into a white dish, pouring melted chocolate over them with such skill that the brown liquid didn't dribble down the side of the jug. With the bowl before her, she nodded her thanks and the waiter moved away, pushing the trolley out of the dining room. Odd, that. He usually visited every table.

Suspicion took hold, twisting in Bishop's mind, a nasty coil of barbed wire that pricked all his senses, putting him on high alert. He stood, casually tugging the hem of his black suit jacket, and walked across the room to the doorway the waiter had gone through. The trolley stood in a corridor, abandoned, all shelves below the top covered with another of those white cloths. He smiled, thinking of every bad action film he'd watched, where a gun-wielding man hid behind the material, ready to pounce.

Double doors with circular glass at the top let him know the kitchen lay behind them and that he didn't have much time. Someone would come out of there in a minute, plate-laden hands held aloft, food piping hot, steam billowing like London fog. He sidled up to the doors and peeked through one of the windows, noting the busy staff in their sauce-stained white uniforms going about their business.

Letting out a sigh of relief, he went back to the trolley and lifted the cloth on one side. Desserts, the same as those on top, filled the two lower shelves—muffins, cheesecakes, and some pastry confection that had God knew what in the middle—but nothing else. He crouched, that barbed wire poking him some more, and shifted a few plates around.

A small jewel bag lay under the lip of a large plate, the requisite black velvet, a drawstring bunching the neck tight. He picked it up and slipped it in the inside pocket of his jacket, standing to settle the cloth back in place. His heart rate accelerated from him having bagged the prize so easily, and he thought about the coming days he would have for free time as a result.

One of the kitchen doors swung open, startling him, although he hid it well. The waiter who had pushed the desserts out here stared at him, mouth dropping open at the same time as his gaze raked over the trolley.

"I took a wrong turn, it seems," Bishop said, his voice, through years of practice, coming out steady and bold.

He turned abruptly and strode back into the dining room, using his peripheral to check whether Miss Jones was still wading through her profiteroles. She'd finished and was sipping from a wine glass half full of water, staring his way. Bishop reached his table and retook his seat, ready to make a swift move if the need arose. He'd chosen this table for the French doors behind him that led out on to a terrace, the edges lined with square marble planters, flowers a riot of colour in the centre and ivy hanging over each corner, the final leaves on each vine kissing the wooden deck. The terrace gave way to a vast lawn, its outskirts boasting tall conifers. This place, in the middle of the English countryside, was the perfect hideaway for what Miss Jones had been contracted to do. For what he'd been contracted to do.

The waiter barged through the doorway, trolley in front of him, and made straight for Fallan's table. He conversed with her, and anyone watching might think nothing untoward was going on, him taking her empty bowl and placing it on the trolley top. She didn't widen her eyes, nor did she exhibit any telling body language. She smiled, nodded, and twisted her wine glass around by the stem.

Oh, she's good.

As the waiter walked away, his strides clipped, his head darting this way and that until his gaze landed on Bishop, Fallan rose. She smoothed down her short black dress—a ridiculous outfit considering the nature of her job—and picked up her red clutch bag from the table. She tucked it under her arm and made her way towards him, hips swaying, those legs of hers going on forever. Lush, full breasts shamelessly sat above a low neckline, giving every man in the room more than an eyeful, and, Bishop suspected, a few lecherous thoughts.

She appeared unaware of the attention she gained—definitely not a woman who knew how appealing she was, how incredibly alluring, and pretty in a sophisticated way—and walked past him without a glance. Her perfume lingered in her wake, a combination of flowers and something spicy he couldn't work out, and he took a deep breath, imagining how intoxicating that aroma would be in a sex-heated room. Cloying. Erotic. Sexy as hell.

Stop thinking about her like that. You've still got work to do. Get it done, then get the fuck out of here.

He knew he should, knew he ought to fulfil his obligations, pack his small bag and check out, taking the goods to his boss. Have a few days off before another assignment came his way. But he couldn't resist getting up and following her, a hound dog chasing the scent, across the terrace and around to the front of the hotel.

She stood leaning against the building beside the semi-circular front steps, talking into a mobile phone. He stopped short, mind whirling with options, and decided on staying where he was, her spotting him be damned. She grew agitated, talking in sharper tones, pressing one hand to her free ear as if she needed to hear better. She nodded, glanced up and spotted him, then muttered something before cutting the call.

He smiled, wanting to put her at ease, but it clearly hadn't worked. She stared at him, eyes wide, that caught-in-the-act face he'd seen too many times to count. He sighed at having such a delicious mark—it made his job more difficult—but he had to take her out whether he found her attractive or not. If he didn't... Well, it just wasn't an option.

In three long strides he was beside her, gripping her elbow and steering her to the other end of the hotel, where darkness cloaked the side of the building and the trees looked nothing more than black blobs against the inky sky. Cloud coverage was nil, and the moon hung behind them, giving him the perfect setting to perform his last task here.

She struggled, quite the hellcat, but didn't say anything, walking beside him until they reached the far corner of the building. He let her go, bracing himself for her to turn more feral, into some kick-arse woman who knew martial arts and could take him down without a second's thought.

She didn't, instead leaning against the hotel, her face hidden by shadow and the night.

"What do you want with me?" she asked.

He savoured her voice — such a shame she wouldn't speak ever again after five minutes with him — and clenched his teeth, knowing what he had to do. Sometimes he hated his job.

"You know what I want, Fallan Jones. Know what I've got to do." He kept his hands by his sides, delaying the inevitable lift and clutch, her neck snapping beneath his grip.

"I...I don't know what you mean," she whispered. "And how do you know my name?"

Very good. She sounded genuine, was quite an actress, and he nodded his approval.

"The bag you put on the dessert trolley." He sniffed, drawing her scent into his nose again.

"What about it?"

He chuckled. She was coming clean, then, giving up the pretence that she didn't know what he wanted with her.

"What's in it?" He guessed jewels — wasn't it always jewels in those bags? — and waited for her answer.

It came quickly. "I don't know. I was told not to look."

Just as he'd expected.

"Who do you work for?" he asked, taking a step closer in case she had a mind to bolt.

"Asda."

He laughed heartily at that. God, she was playing the game right until the end, wasn't she? Asda...couldn't she have picked a shop a little more upmarket? Waitrose, at least?

"It's a job," she snapped. "It pays the bills."

"I'm sure it does. What about your other employer?"

She snorted. "You think I have time for a second job? I work all the hours God sends as it is. What do you want with me? I phoned someone back there, and when you came along I told him. You'll get caught for whatever you're thinking of doing, the man told me that."

He ignored her, unperturbed by the threat. "You must earn a good whack to be able to afford to stay here and wear a dress that must have cost two weeks' wages working for *Asda*..."

"I won this weekend away! What has it got to do with you, anyway?"

He had to guess, what with the darkness, but he'd bet she was looking at him now, mutinous, angry.

"It has everything to do with me. You're lying. Who do you work for?" He snatched her wrist up, squeezing with enough pressure to let her know he meant business but not enough to leave a bruise.

Not that it mattered. She'd be dead in a few minutes. A pity, that.

"I told you!"

She tried to wrench her arm free and, failing, sagged against the wall. He wished he could see her face, read her expression, but perhaps it was just as well he couldn't. He might well start believing her.

He sighed. "You know what happens now, don't you?"

"What?" she asked, that one word spoken with the first hint of hysteria. "Please, I don't know what you're talking about. And you're hurting me. You have me mixed up with someone else."

He laughed again, quietly this time. Didn't they always say that? Wasn't that the general patter they came out with every time he caught up with them? A script that every mark was instructed to use, taking their true identity—and that of their employers—with them to the grave?

A shuffle to their right brought him up short. He should have expected it. The waiter would have passed a message on by now, and whoever had booked a night here in order to collect that bag would be on the lookout for him. He glanced to the side, tightening his hold on her, and saw a retreating black movement—someone's shadow following the person it was tagged to. Whoever had peered around the side of the building had stepped back out of sight after making the mistake of creating noise.

"Come with me."

Bishop made for the hotel's rear, dragging Fallan behind him. She stumbled several times trying to keep up with him, pulling against his hold, tiny whimpers coming out of her. He forced himself to remember she was acting, that she'd been paid to do just this, and made her walk faster. Once at his car, he shoved her inside, strapping her into the passenger seat.

"Don't even think about getting out."

She stared up at him, eyes full of fear, and he almost felt sorry for her. Maybe she was new to this game. Maybe this was her first job. Whatever, it shouldn't matter to him, shouldn't be something he even thought about, but he had and would have to address that when he had some downtime. Marks weren't supposed to get to you. Marks were meant to be removed from the equation — quickly, easily, no mess. Marks weren't meant to sit in your bloody car and look at you in that way, melting the ice around your damn heart until you convinced yourself they were telling the truth.

Fuck it!

He slammed the door, rounded the bonnet and climbed into the driver's side. With the engine revving, he swerved out of his parking space, making a mental note to call the hotel in the morning and check out. They could send along his bag containing a few changes of clothes, toothbrush, deodorant and shower gel, but, then again, it might be safer if they didn't. There was nothing he needed desperately, nothing he'd mind being without. The waiter having something to do with this... No, they could keep his bag and send it to the address he'd booked in with.

Out on the main road, Fallan silent beside him, he eased his foot to the floor, conscious of the pinprick headlights behind them. If he put his mind to it, he'd lose that bastard and take Fallan to his flat in London, deal with her there and have his boss send someone to remove her body.

"I heard that if you do as you're told," she said quietly, "an abductor is less likely to kill you."

He frowned, eyeing the rear-view mirror again. What the fuck had made her say that? "I heard that if you work for dodgy outfits, you're more likely to get killed than if you worked for a company like, say, Asda."

He wanted to laugh again but held it back, concentrating on the distance between his car and the one behind. It was gaining on him. *Fuck.*

"I swear," she said, "I don't know what you mean. I won that break away. Won it!"

"How? Where did you apply?" He may as well humour her.

"It was a treasure hunt thing. Offer came through the post. Several people each won a weekend away at different locations, and each of us had to hide some treasure. Shit, I wish I'd never applied now, but I couldn't afford a holiday and it seemed the perfect thing to do. And I didn't expect to win. Didn't think I had a cat in hell's chance and I—"

"Be quiet." He needed to think. Either she was a pro or she was telling the truth.

Something inside him leaned towards the latter.

Jesus Christ, this is all I need. Some innocent caught up in this crap.

He gritted his teeth, jaw muscles pulsing, and looked in the rear-view again.

The car was getting closer.

Chapter Two

Great, just great. Fallan should have known — bloody should have *known* the whole weekend away thing would be a scam. One look at her insanely handsome kidnapper told her she was in fucking trouble.

She looked out of the car window and watched the lights go by, her Beef Wellington and mound of profiteroles sitting heavy in her stomach. The delicious meal had gone down a treat. How could something so simple turn into a nightmare?

A treasure hunt, and she'd been told not to inspect the contents of the bag. As an employee at Asda, she knew not to look a gift horse in the mouth. All she'd needed to do was participate by leaving the bag at a location, enjoying the meal and then the hotel's facilities. Why, then, was the man at her side treating her as if she was part of some *Mission: Impossible* film production?

The only thing she usually had to look forward to was work — at least it got her out of the house — and the latest hint of excitement was when a five-year-old had dropped and smashed a jar of piccalilli on the shop floor. Cleaning the yellow mess had been the highlight of her week up until this.

"Please tell me why you're taking me?" she asked.

"I just told you to be quiet."

She decided to keep him talking. "Well, if you knew anything about me or most women in general you'd know that in high-tension situations we panic. Not only that, I've been known to talk a lot, so me being quiet isn't really an option." She rubbed her sweaty palms down her thighs.

She glanced over at him. He was so bloody handsome…and what was she doing thinking something like that in a situation like this?

That's it, Fallan, start getting the hots for your kidnapper. Isn't there a name for that type of thing?

Nothing good would come out of this experience. That knowledge hit her hard, and she filtered through her options. She couldn't get out of the car—he'd child-locked it—and even if she could he was going too fast for her to get out without seriously hurting herself. But that didn't matter, did it? Not when she risked being harmed in a worse way if she stayed with him.

Suddenly he swerved to miss another car coming in the opposite direction, flinging her against the door.

"Are you fucking insane?" she screamed.

"Be quiet."

His demands were angering her by the second.

"Are you crazy? Did you just escape some loony bin and decided to pick on me?" She glared at him.

"In case you haven't noticed, we're being followed."

Followed? Fallan glanced behind her at what looked like a black van travelling at normal speed, nothing suspicious.

"Are you sure you're feeling okay?" she asked, reaching out to touch his temple, unable to stop the sarcasm filtering into her voice.

Do as he says and be quiet. You'll get yourself in more trouble by pissing him off.

He caught her wrist in one movement. "Try anything and I can break your bones faster than you can think." He applied a little pressure before he let her go.

"Ow. I was only trying to care." She nursed her wrist and glared at him again.

"Don't."

He was constantly checking out the van in his rear-view mirror. She looked back and again saw no need to panic. It was just a van…with occupants who could help her…

Shaking her head, she turned away from him, releasing a long, heavy sigh.

So much for a wonderful time away.

"Who are you?" he asked.

"I told you, my name is Fallan Jones and I work at Asda. I'm no one."

"Here, take this."

He handed her something heavy and metal. Turning it over, she glanced at the device in her hand and screamed.

"Are you fucking mental? That's a gun!" She dropped it on the floor, at the same time realising she'd had the upper hand when she'd held it. *Shit.*

Fallan no longer cared if she plunged to her death while leaping out of his moving vehicle. She had to get away from this man who was intent on scaring the shit out of her.

"Let me out, fucking let me out!" Pulling on the lever did no good. After a few seconds she gave up and decided to spend the entire journey glaring at him. Not a massive hardship, all things considered. Yes, he had a long scar down the side of his face but it didn't detract from his gorgeousness.

"You've never seen a gun?" he asked.

"Last time I checked at work, we weren't selling crap that could kill. Besides, with our high crime rate, I fail to see why selling guns for anyone and everyone to use would be productive to the nation."

"You really aren't a killer, are you?"

"I don't know about that. I accidentally killed my goldfish. I cried for weeks."

He cursed and swerved as the black van overtook them. She watched it pass, hoping to catch the driver's attention, but the windows were blacked out.

They drove for another few minutes. Fallan kept staring at him, refusing to look away. Every now and then he glanced over at her before returning his focus to the road.

"You know, you staring is distracting," he said.

"Then keep your eyes on the road. Pretend I'm not here."

"While you keep your eyes on me?"

"Look, pal, buddy, criminal—whatever you want to call yourself. I have no idea why the hell I'm here, what the hell you think I've done, but I'm certainly not who you think I am. And, while we're at it, what's your name?"

He ignored her.

"Please can I go home?"

"Bishop."

Fallan frowned. "What does a chess piece have to do with this?"

"My name is Bishop."

Oh. An unusual name, not that she could talk, but she doubted it was real. Not for a first name, anyway, and if it was, his parents had weird ideas.

"Whatever. Can I go home?"

"I don't think home will be suitable for you."

Fallan shook her head and gave up trying to reason with the man. She turned away and gave outside her full attention, thinking about the trip she'd been offered and the promised money coming after the treasure hunt.

How many times had her mother said nothing came in this world for free? She should have known.

"You've gone quiet," he said.

"I don't feel like talking now."

"I thought you said you talked a lot."

Sighing, she turned back to him. "I talk to people I like, and, in the few minutes we've known each other, I've decided I don't like you. Funny, that. I mean, I must have been nuts to think I could like someone who kidnapped me from the only chance I'll get for having a weekend away anytime in the next decade. Thanks for that. Really appreciate it. Just do what you've got to do and then take me home. Hurt me, whatever, just get it over and done with. I bet you're with that Frankie Lash bloke, aren't you? He said if I looked in the bag it wouldn't 'bode well' for me. Except I didn't look in the bag — like I would after he'd said something like that — and I needed the ten grand he offered for playing in the treasure hunt."

He widened his eyes and stared at her for a second or two. "Frankie Lash? Treasure hunt?"

"Yes. I had to put the bag on the trolley and —"

"Oh, fuck."

"What?"

"Nothing. I can't take you home."

"Whatever."

"You say that a lot."

"You know, for a man who keeps asking me to be quiet, you're asking an awful lot of questions, which then makes me have to answer."

Bishop went silent. Fallan smiled. Ten minutes in his company and she was already driving him crazy. If she kept this up, he'd be glad to dump her at the earliest opportunity.

A brief turn into a narrow lane and Bishop stopped the car and shut off the lights.

"What are you doing?" she asked.

Bishop grabbed her jacket and slammed his lips on hers. The move was so unexpected Fallan didn't respond. She struggled to get away from him, but, pressed up against the window as she was, she couldn't move. He pushed his tongue through and, before she knew what was happening, she was kissing him back. He tasted good, but she was fucked if she'd let him just take what he wanted.

A knock on the window snapped them apart. She gasped, heart thumping wildly, and sat straight, her lips sore from his light stubble.

"If you speak, or scream, or do anything to fuck this up, I'll kill you." Bishop pressed a button and the window moved down, the squeaking noise loud against the sound of her breathing.

Licking her lips, she darted a glance at Bishop. His lips were shiny and looked as swollen as hers felt.

"What are you two doing here?" A policeman shone a torch on both of them.

She just had to speak out, to tell him she'd been taken against her will, but Bishop laid one hand on her thigh and squeezed. The officer obviously saw something else in the action as he snorted and directed the beam at Bishop.

"I'm sorry, Officer, but this fine woman at my side just agreed to be my wife, so we stopped and... Well, sorry, we shouldn't have."

Fallan widened her eyes, then smiled, even though it felt forced and fake. "What can I say, a *dangerous*-looking man is always someone I like being kissed by in a lane in the middle of nowhere when I'd much rather be home." *Please let him realise what I mean, please...*

Bishop squeezed her thigh harder.

"Well, move it on," the officer said. "I don't want to have to charge you two with indecent behaviour." He slammed a palm on the roof then stepped back to wave them off.

Bishop closed the window, started the car and reversed out of the lane.

She stared at the officer, pleading with her eyes, but he only nodded then returned to his motorbike.

"What did I tell you?" Bishop asked.

"That if I said anything you'd —"

"Do you have a death wish?"

"I wasn't aware I had one, but it seems I do, yes."

"I saw the policeman pull up back there," he said. "I needed to create a distraction and kissing you was the only thing I could come up with."

"Oh," she said, getting ready to give him a heavy dose of sarcasm, "and there was me thinking I was irresistible."

"Be quiet."

She obeyed this time. Several minutes later he pulled up alongside a river.

"Are you going to kill me? Dump me in there?" Despite her strong voice, she was panicking inside.

She unbuckled her seatbelt and scrambled for the lock, knowing it was futile but going with her instincts.

Bishop placed his arm across her chest and pushed her back in her seat. The strength from his move terrified her.

"I don't kill women after I've just kissed them. Besides, I don't think you're who I thought you were. But I still can't take you home."

Fallan raised her hand and slapped him across the face. "Don't you dare talk to me as though what you've done is nothing. I haven't done anything wrong, and you can tell that to Frankie Lash. I did what he said and I want my ten grand." She rubbed her palm, which stung and felt like it was going to bruise.

He ran his fingers over the spot she'd slapped then cursed, getting out of the car.

Taking a deep breath, Fallan watched him stand by the river, her nerves jumping all over the place. It was cold now that the heater wasn't on.

"Go out there and talk to him," she whispered.

The worst he could do was throw her in the river. Unless he had another gun on him. It reminded her of the one on the floor and she picked it up and got out of the car on his side. The deathtrap in her hands was heavy and scary to hold.

"You've brought a friend with you," he said, without turning to face her.

She lifted the gun. The heavy weight made her hands shake. "I don't want to die."

He turned round. "You really think you can use that?"

"You don't know who I am." If he thought she was someone else she may as well act like it.

"Yes, I do. You're Fallan Jones, shelf-filler for Asda." With each word he moved closer and closer until he stood with his chest pressed against the business end of the gun.

He was right, she didn't even know if she could use it. Could she take a life even with the threat to her own?

Bishop grabbed her arm, took the gun and spun her around with her back to his chest. He pointed the gun at her temple.

"What are you doing?" she cried, legs almost giving out on her.

"Pointing a gun at someone gets questions answered. Now tell me about this trip."

She felt sick, didn't know if she'd be able to speak, but she'd give it a damn good try. "I got it through the post. Some kind of special treasure hunt game. No one playing was to talk about it and you got paid ten grand once you'd been on the weekend, delivered the bag, and returned home. I was visited by someone who ordered me not to look in the bag, said if I did it wouldn't go down too well and I wouldn't qualify for the money. Frankie Lash, he said his name was, and that I'd need to remember that name if I didn't follow the rules because he wasn't called Lash for nothing." All the secrets she knew she shouldn't be telling came spilling out. She'd lose the money now if that Lash man found out.

"Who else spoke to you?"

"Only Frankie. He was scary as hell, even though he smiled and acted nicely. I knew I shouldn't have agreed once I met him, but… I need the money… I don't want to die. Please. I only thought it was a bit of fun."

Tears streamed, and the very real knowledge that this guy pointing a gun at her could end her life within seconds slammed into her.

I'm going to be sick...

"Just so you know, I don't kill women unless they're on my list. Congratulations, Fallan Jones, this is your lucky day." He kissed her cheek and let her go. "Oh, and by the way, this isn't loaded. You wouldn't have killed anyone." Bishop tucked the gun inside his jacket.

Fallan's temper spiked. "You bastard. Threatening me and doing that."

She lunged forward, intent on scratching his face, pummelling him with her fists, anything to hurt him, but he grabbed her arm and pulled her to the car.

"I suggest you get in the car because you're not out of the clear yet. You have Mr Lash to worry about. He's...an undesirable man. *He'd* kill you without a second's thought."

Fallan didn't argue. Her life and safety were now in this man's hands.

* * * *

Some time later, Fallan sat at a table in a kitchen. She didn't know where it was. Bishop had blindfolded her for the journey. Once they'd arrived here, he'd chained her hands to the seat back. Shaking her head, she thought about her life again. What had she done wrong? Was this all part of the holiday resort test? Some new addition she wasn't aware of? Was it their way of getting out of paying her the ten grand? If she spilled, she didn't get it? Were all the other players going through the same thing?

"Okay, we're going to start again. Name?" he asked.

"Mickey Mouse," she mumbled, then, seeing the dark look he gave her, said, "Fallan Jones."

"Occupation?"

"Drug dealer." *Stop it!*

"Fallan, I know this must be annoying to you but just try to give me the right answers. I know you've told me this before, but I have to make sure you really are who you say you are."

She glared at him, lips pressed together.

He sighed. "I tell you what, I'll find out for myself."

He click-click-clicked on a laptop, bringing up what looked like a file. If he'd done a search on her, he'd have found out she was just a boring, everyday girl.

"Where are we?" she asked.

"In my safe house."

"Oh, a safe house. Sounds so movie-ish." She rolled her eyes.

Silence met her statement. Bishop clearly had issues with women who spoke their minds.

"I need to use the bathroom," she said.

"Hold it."

"I've been holding it. I need to use the bathroom."

"Like I said, hold it."

"And like *I* said, I have been."

He ignored her. She glared at him, hating the fact he was so good-looking. Hating herself for even thinking it.

A few seconds later the laptop beeped and he closed it.

"So you're Fallan Jones, Asda employee, and your mother died last year of cancer. You wanted the ten grand because you're in debt from donating money to the hospital while she was ill. Hoping some medical cure would help in time? You dropped out of university two years ago to care for her. You're twenty-four."

"Wow, you got all that from a computer? Congrats, whiz-kid. I bet you were the computer geek in high school." Fallan rattled her chains. "I've got to go to the bathroom."

"Why else did you decide to do this treasure hunt?"

"I need the money. The house is about to be taken off me by the bank. I need to make a significant payment so that doesn't happen. We fell behind on the mortgage while Mum was ill. Do you want me to continue?" The need of the money shamed her. She rattled the chains even more.

"Don't try anything funny," he warned, walking towards her.

"You've put a gun to my temple, threatened me at every turn. You know a lot more about me than I do about you. Please, just let me use the fucking bathroom."

Bishop unlocked the cuffs, leaving them dangling on each wrist, but led her to the bathroom, shut and locked the door, leaned his back against it and crossed his arms.

"What are you doing?" she asked, outraged.

"Do your business."

"I'm not doing it in front of you."

"Either do it or I'll chain you back to the chair and you can piss there."

"This is embarrassing." Pulling her dress up to her waist, she followed by pushing down her tights. Before she touched her panties, she glared at him. "Won't you give me *some* privacy? At least turn around."

Bishop snorted but faced the door. She blushed as she looked at his back and tight arse. His trousers enhanced the powerful muscles beneath, and, God help her, her body was melting to feel him underneath her hands.

She shoved those thoughts away. Once she'd done her business and washed her hands, Bishop was watching her again.

"You do realise you're in a shitload of trouble," he said.

Fallan shook her head. "No! I had no idea! Of course I realise I'm in a shitload of fucking trouble, but I followed instructions and now I'm here. I just hope the other women were lucky."

"Other women. Tell me about them."

"About a group of ten, I think. We each got a different location. Some abroad and some stayed near home." She sniffed and got a whiff of her body odour. "Just out of curiosity, will I be allowed a shower?"

"Yes. With me."

"Wait a minute. This is a complete breach of my privacy, not to mention how unfair you're being."

Bishop pressed her up against the wall. She couldn't turn away from his intense stare.

"Fallan Jones, you've signed on for an adventure of a lifetime. I know you want me. If that copper hadn't come along…" He caught her wrist as she was about to slap his face. "I'll let you get away with one, not two, darling, so you'd better put those little claws away." He moved his hands down to her breasts. She gasped, outraged yet excited to have him do what he wanted with her body.

"Don't touch me," she protested, even though it sounded weak.

"You want me, Fallan. Don't you?"

He kissed her and she knew she'd been caught. Moaning, she wanted to touch him everywhere.

Bishop swept her hair off her face, tilted her chin and deepened the kiss. Then he pulled back, leaving her breathless.

"You taste like sweet honey," he said.

Her senses on high alert, she had the urge to wind her hands round his neck. She wanted to feel his thick hair between her fingers. The rattle of the cuffs brought her out of her semi-erotic haze.

"I don't want you. I'd never want a man like you."

Bishop chuckled. Fallan was sure she saw disappointment in his eyes before he turned away. Seeing the streak of real emotion, she felt guilty. The mysterious Bishop had been the first to really open up the woman inside her.

"I'm sorry," she whispered, not sure if he'd heard her at all. Closing her eyes, she cursed her body and her reactions to this man.

"Like I said, you want me."

Chapter Three

Waterman choked on his Earl Grey. It went down the wrong hole, and the resulting coughing fit lasted quite some time. At one point he thought he wasn't going to be able to breathe, and he smacked the side of his fist on his chest, mentally cursing for swallowing wrong and showing a weaker side of himself. It was never a good thing to let your guard down in front of your employees, to have them know you were in any way vulnerable, but there was nothing he could do about that now. What was done was done, so to speak, and he'd have to deal with it.

The coughing eased, and he looked ahead through watery eyes. Kemp stood in front of Waterman's desk, and Frankie lounged in a chair beside him, seemingly unperturbed. Neither offered their services of a pat on the back. Waterman didn't like fuss, and, unless he was dying, those two could stay the fuck back and they knew it.

Once suitably composed, Waterman wiped his eyes with the back of his hand and took another sip of tea to ease his now-sore throat. He placed the white bone china cup on the matching saucer and eyed the men opposite. They were his best blokes, but at the moment he wondered whether he would be better off recruiting new blood. These two were getting on a bit, going stale. He took his attention off them and stared at the green leather blotter on his desk, mulling over how to sort out this mess.

"So," he said, "say that again, Frankie. But slower. I need to make sure I heard you right."

Frankie squirmed. Kemp looked smug.

"One of the women is with a government goon," Frankie said, sitting straighter and holding both hands up as if to ward Waterman off should he decide to lunge forward. "I telephoned each of our collectors to make sure all the packages had been hidden then picked up, like you said, but there's been a hitch."

"A hitch," Waterman stated. "A fucking hitch. I don't do hitches, do I? Go on."

Frankie cleared his throat. "Our bloke who was going to pick the package up at the hotel a few miles down the road—"

Waterman sucked in a breath then released it slowly. "Which one, fuck-face? We've got several hotels on our list that are a few miles down the fucking road." He clamped his lips together to stop himself calling Frankie a useless bastard. He wasn't scared of him, could handle himself if he had to, but Frankie had a reputation for being a right hard fucker and Waterman didn't fancy being on the end of his fist tonight.

"The Hidden Gem," Frankie said.

"The Hidden fucking Gem," Waterman said, chuckling without mirth. He was livid and having a hard job hiding it. That hotel hadn't sat right with him when he'd arranged this job, but the client had insisted on it. "Right, well, what the hell happened?" He glanced at Kemp, who stared right back with an I-told-you-so expression. "Fuck you, Kemp. Carry on, Frankie."

"We sent our man to collect, but someone else got there first."

Waterman grimaced. "I thought that's what you said the first time, but you know how it is. I needed you to say it again in case I was going a bit deaf, like. Got a bead on who took the cargo and how he even knew it was there?"

Frankie puffed out his chest. "Yep on the bead. Our man followed the car containing the lifter and the woman. Took down the number plate."

"Which is?" Waterman leant forward to take a slip of paper from Frankie. He glared at the numbers and letters scrawled on it. "It's that fucking wanker again, isn't it? Using the same damn car, the cheeky bastard." He held back from slamming his fist onto the desk. "I'm still pissed off we haven't caught up with him from the last time he poked his hooter in where it wasn't wanted." He paused, looking at the ceiling, making a note to get the painters in. His cigar smoke had turned it off-white. "Remind me of the woman's name." He didn't need telling. Just wanted to see if Frankie knew his arse from his elbow, whether he was still as sharp as he had been in the past.

"Fallan Jones. Needed the money cos her old dear dying of cancer made her a bit skint. Stands to lose her house."

"Stands to lose her fucking legs if she opens her gob," Waterman said. "So our man...*lost* them, is that right?"

"Yeah. One minute the car was in front of him, the next, gone." Frankie leant back and pinched his chin, flicking his tongue behind his bottom teeth.

Waterman wanted to punch him. "Just like that, eh? Marvellous." He took another sip of tea, enjoying the sound of cup base meeting saucer as he placed the drink back down. "Reckon he'll be looking for a new job by now. Knows I won't tolerate that crap. Put his name in my little book there, so if he comes knocking on my door asking for sympathy I can tell him to stick his request where the sun don't fucking shine." He propped his elbows on his desk and linked his fingers, resting his chin on top. "So, we need to find the woman. Been to her house yet?"

Frankie nodded. "No one at home."

"Got someone posted outside?" *Please tell me you used your brain, dickhead.*

"Yep." Frankie wiggled in his seat, clearly proud of himself.

"Good. Kemp, your job's to find that wanker who took the goods. We know he uses aliases, has some gaff he hides away in, but now we know he's using the same car we might get lucky. See if that bastard at the city CCTV place can help us out, too. Might catch sight of his car on video."

"He said he couldn't last time I asked," Kemp said. "Something about his bosses getting suspicious."

"I don't give a toss what he said or what he's going to say." Waterman took a cigar from the wooden box in front of him and toyed with it. "You just remind him we know where he lives, where his wife works, and where his kids go to school."

"I did that before but—"

"Then do it a-fucking-gain!" *So help me God, I'll shoot you right now if you argue with me anymore.*

"Right, Guv."

"So," Waterman said on a sigh. "Like I said, you're on finding that wanker."

"Continuing the search for him and failing, you mean." Kemp smirked.

Waterman pointed at him, jabbing his finger in the air. "If you're not fucking careful, mate, you'll find yourself at the bottom of the Thames wearing a new pair of cement shoes. That mouth of yours is starting to get on my nerves, know what I mean?"

Kemp blushed and shuffled from foot to foot.

"Get to it, lads. There's a lot of money riding on this, and, until you come up with the goods, you're losing out. I won't pay up until we have all those bags back. Oh, and Frankie? You need to give that dopey bastard a warning—the one who lost that wanker and the woman. Let him know how the land lies, right?"

Frankie nodded and he and Kemp left the room. Waterman picked up the phone and issued an order for Kemp to be tailed. That little fucker had been pushing his buttons for too long now. Getting too big for his boots, he was.

Waterman didn't do people getting too big for their boots.

* * * *

Bishop leaned his back to the cold tiled wall of the shower while Fallan stood beneath the spray, facing away from him. There was no way he could hide his hard cock—no way he wanted to, either. There was something about her that made him act differently, like when he'd told her he knew she wanted him. Although he sensed she did, he had no idea why he'd said so. That wasn't his usual style. The lack of sex must be getting to him. The last time he'd had a 'usual style' was too far in the past to remember, and, if Fallan was under any illusion he didn't want *her*, she'd only have to turn and face him and he wouldn't have to say a fucking word.

He took in the sight of her shapely arse and the way her thighs tapered to slim calves and even slimmer ankles. She had a good body on her, he'd give her that, and the glimpse he'd had of her tits when she'd climbed into the shower was all he'd needed to send his dick bolt upright.

It wasn't fair that men didn't get to hide their arousal.

Was she turned on with him in here with her? When he'd kissed her, she'd been breathless, clinging on to him as if they weren't in any jeopardy at all, were just on a date where they'd progressed to the next level after dinner. Maybe the danger of their situation had made her needy...horny even. Who knew? He thought about that as she soaped herself, thick bubbles gliding over places he longed to touch himself.

He never thought he'd wish he were lather.

Could he fuck her knowing she might only allow him to through fear? Or, worse, to get him on side, make him drop his guard so she could slip away when he was having a weak moment? No, he couldn't, no matter how much his cock protested now, throbbing like a son of a bitch, announcing that it needed touching, needed to be inside her.

If she wanted a fuck, she'd have to ask for it, make it clear she was up for it. He'd laid the groundwork and it was up to her to start building the frame. If he pushed her he might lose her. That wasn't something he fancied contemplating. She'd already got under his skin in a way no other woman had, and the thought of not fucking her left him oddly empty inside. He hadn't felt like that since…well, in a long time.

"I know you're looking at me," she said, tipping her head back so the water soaked her face.

Yeah, he was looking at her all right—difficult not to when they were about two feet apart. Fuck, his bollocks ached.

"And?" He waited for a typical female response—the kind he'd got from other women who'd wanted to get into his pants but denied it.

"So stop it. I need to turn around so I can get my hair wet then wash it. You have to close your eyes."

"Do I now?"

"Yes, you do."

"And you're going to make me, how?"

She tensed, her shoulders going rigid, fingertips appearing over her shoulders as she crossed her arms over her breasts. "I can't make you. I just thought you might do the gentlemanly thing and give me some privacy, despite being in here with me, which, as I said before when I used the toilet, is a total violation."

"All right. Turn around." He closed his eyes.

"Have you closed your eyes?"

"Yes."

"Because I don't want to be turning around to find you gawping at me."

"You're safe."

"Are you sure?"

"What, am I sure I've got my eyes closed and I'm not staring at your sexy arse? Fuck yes, I'm sure."

The squeak of her feet sounded as she undoubtedly faced him.

"Oh!"

She'd seen his cock, then.

"Like what you see?" he asked, dying to peek at her.

"Um, I... Um. No, I don't."

"Liar." *What the hell's wrong with you, talking to her like that?*

"I'm not in the habit of lying."

Was she staring at him? Taking her fill? Did she want to reach out and grasp him? Kneel to suck his dick?

If only she would...

"There's a first time for everything, Fallan, and that was your first time."

"God, you insufferable bastard! You've got a high opinion of yourself, haven't you?"

He knew he came across that way but couldn't help himself from blurting what was in his mind regarding her. She'd sent him off-kilter, her presence grabbing him by the bollocks and holding on tight ever since he'd seen her eating that damn Beef Wellington.

"Not really," he said. "Have you washed your hair yet?"

"No, so keep your eyes closed until I have."

He held back a smile at her issuing orders. Given her situation, he thought she'd have been a bit more obedient, but she had a mouth on her and seemed to feel confident she could speak to him that way.

He liked a strong woman.

He heard her squeezing shampoo out and imagined it filling her palm—imagined how her hair would feel if he washed it for her. He almost pushed off the wall, opened his eyes and took over the job, but somehow he didn't think she'd appreciate that.

Not yet.

The scent of vanilla and honey wafted around him, strong and refreshing. Despite the heat from the steam he was feeling a little cold and, thinking maybe she had her eyes closed as she massaged her head, he opened his a touch to see how long she'd be before he could change places with her.

Fuck. He shouldn't have done that. She had her head back, water pattering over her hair and sending lather down her body in a sensual, creamy swathe. His cock hardened further at the sight of bubbles coasting over her sopping breasts then down, getting caught on the curls between her legs. She was a fine woman to look at, even finer to be around. He could get attached in no time, but if he didn't think before he spoke in future she'd continue to see him as an arrogant prick she wanted nothing to do with.

"Finished yet?" he asked, closing his eyes again.

"No."

"Only, I need a shower myself."

"Then you'll just have to wait your turn."

"Right." He sighed. "Any idea how long you'll be?"

"As long as it takes."

She was enjoying this, he was sure of it.

"So if I told you to get a fucking move on because we need to catch some sleep before hightailing it out of here before the sun comes up—before someone comes to find us—you reckon you'd still be taking your time?"

"I'll… Shit, I've just got to condition…"

He smiled. They had time, and plenty of it. No one but his boss knew of this location. Fallan didn't need to know that, though.

He thought about her earlier request to go home. He understood her need, but she didn't quite realise who they were dealing with. Frankie Lash wasn't someone to piss off, and the guy he worked for, Waterman, was another to be avoided at all costs. Bishop was still keeping out of Waterman's way. The man was narked at Bishop for working for him undercover and getting information on every job Waterman had done in the past. Bishop's boss had wanted it as insurance — bribery to ensure Waterman stayed within the boundaries of crime acceptability — and so far it had worked. Bishop had grown a beard for that job, an itchy motherfucker he'd been glad to eventually shave off once his mission was complete — or, to be exact, when it had gone tits up.

But Waterman never forgot a face, never forgot the shape of a man's eyes, he'd said once, and Bishop had been glad he'd worn coloured contact lenses. Even though Bishop was sure he'd covered his arse on absolutely everything, he still got the jitters from time to time, still looked over his shoulder, knowing Waterman wouldn't let him just walk off into the sunset. Now Waterman's outfit was connected to this job, Bishop was in no doubt he'd have to cross paths with them again...and possibly be recognised one way or another.

Fuck.

"Okay, I've finished," Fallan said. "Keep your eyes closed while we switch places."

This should be interesting...

He shoved off the wall and took a step forward, hand out to his right so he had something to touch and gain his bearings. The tiles were wet with condensation, silky like he imagined her slit would be. Her body heat reached him before she did, warming his front, and he held his breath while she brushed past him. The skin-on-skin contact set his cock to throbbing, but, before he'd fully registered that her stomach — or was it her side? — had come into contact with him, she was gone.

"You can open your eyes now," she said. "I'm behind you."

He opened them and moved under the spray. "Do you have *your* eyes closed?"

"No, I don't."

"Oh, so it's okay for you to look at *my* arse while *I'm* showering, but I can't—"

"Oh, be quiet. It isn't the same."

"It isn't?"

"No, I don't want to look at you. I'm actually staring at the plughole."

He roared with laughter then asked, "Not my arse?"

"What, that hairy thing?"

"How do you know it's hairy if you're not looking?" He smiled, enjoying their conversation.

"I don't, I'm just guessing."

"Well, you guessed wrong. It isn't hairy." He soaped his body.

"It so is!"

"Gotcha."

"Oh…sod off!"

Bishop continued to shower in the silence that followed, turning around without embarrassment to let the water sluice down his back. He washed his front again, paying particular attention to his cock, making it harder and loving the sound of her sharp intake of air and the way she stared wide-eyed at every move he made.

She doesn't want me, my arse.

Chapter Four

Why, of all people, did this have to happen to her? A gorgeous guy—no, the sexiest man she'd ever met—was showering right in front of her and, rather than being angry about the situation, she was busy drooling over his dick.

No matter how hard she tried, Fallan couldn't tear her gaze away. His cock was long and thick, and a vein throbbed at the side, the foreskin pulling back each time he dragged his hand down the large shaft.

Mouth watering, pussy creaming, Fallan moved forward.

What the hell am I doing?

She checked to make sure his eyes were closed then took a step back.

"I don't mind you getting closer," he said, startling her. His eyes were still closed.

"How did you know…? I mean, I don't know what you're talking about!"

"Baby, I know a desperate woman when I see one and I bet you're hungry for a thick, hard cock." He cupped his balls with his free hand while his other stroked the head.

"That's not fair. You're masturbating." She covered her mouth with her hand.

Stop talking, Fallan. This man abducted you and is now trying to get you to have sex with him.

You want to have sex with him.

Do not.

Do too. Come on, it'll be dangerous, hot and totally worth it.

Fisting her hands, Fallan spun away, presenting him with her back. She rested her head on the wall, one palm flat out beside her head, and hiked in great breaths of air trying to ease her mind, clear her erotic thoughts and calm the fuck down.

Don't think of him — think about the mounting debt, the mortgage, the funeral bills, the mundane job serving customers behind the tills and listening to their moaning when they can't find anything.

If she had her way, she wouldn't be fucking working on a till.

All this is your fault, Mum.

Fallan shut off the hurt and betrayal, the guilt at what she'd just thought. If her mother were alive, she'd know what to do. But she couldn't think like that. Her mother was dead and she was all alone, and her mother had hardly signed up for cancer, eager to have it ravage her body and take her away. Fallan had no one now, and at the present time nobody would be aware she was gone. Her boss would when she didn't turn up, but employees came and went there all the time. It wouldn't be anything unusual.

I shouldn't have taken the holiday.

Bishop gripped her by the shoulders and spun her around, pressing her back against the cold, tiled wall.

A tall and naked Bishop who did things to her she had no business experiencing. Not like this, not here, in this situation. But this man called to her. She'd been with men for sex before. She wasn't all that into relationships but she liked a good, hard fucking. Fallan guessed it was the only rebellious thing about her.

"What are you doing?" she asked, not caring as her pussy leaked cream and her tummy muscles tightened. She stuck her breasts out, the nipples budding—a deliberate invitation for him to take her so she could get on his good side. She wanted to feel his teeth nipping at her hard teats, his cock in her cunt, pumping into her until she came so hard she saw stars.

Anything to make her forget where she was for a moment and why she was here.

"I thought you said you didn't want me?" he said.

"I don't," she lied.

Fuck me, fuck me. Don't ask me for permission, just take me.

Being kidnapped must have gone straight to her head. She never allowed any man to take from her— she was the person who took—but the idea of him doing what he wanted while she pretended his attentions weren't welcome turned her the hell on.

What's the matter with you?

"I bet your pussy is nice and wet." Bishop pressed against her, his cock pushing into her belly.

"It's not." Fallan bit her lip—her biggest lie of all.

He moved a strand of hair away from her face and caressed a path down her chest, over her breasts, past her stomach to cup her swollen, wet heat. Her light dusting of curls was already soaked—not by water now but by her juice, but he didn't need to know that.

She didn't push him away. She didn't fight. Instead, she opened her legs wider to receive him, silently urging him forward.

"I won't go any further until you ask me to." He pulled his hand away and turned from her, exiting the shower to pick up a towel.

"Excuse me?" she panted. Her heart fluttered and her entire body was a full ball of need.

He turned his back on her. "You heard me. Either tell me what you want or you don't get to fuck."

The ultimatum spoken, Fallan cursed the blush creeping into her cheeks. He'd struck out first and like a fool she'd let him.

"What do you want me to say?" Fallan couldn't maintain the fight much longer. How could she deny what she so obviously wanted?

"You've got a couple of options," he said. "You can say, 'Leave me alone' or, 'Bishop, fuck me.'"

His words enraged and inflamed her, yet at the same time they melted her further.

Would he be vocal during sex?

Only one way to find out. Fallan might well be making a mistake, but she refused to think about that now. Life and everything waiting for her at home was boring. She worked, went home, ate and cleaned, went to bed and got up to start the mundane routine again. With it came worries that she was working for a pittance, money that barely covered the bills let alone the debts mounting by the minute. She was fucked, yes, but she wanted to be in an entirely different way.

Before her stood a man with a large cock presenting her with an opportunity to take what she wanted from life for a change. The consequences could wait until later. All she needed was to utter a few simple words to get what she wanted, to take herself to a place where nothing mattered, where worries and upset didn't exist.

In the boldest move of her life, she stepped out of the shower, walked to him and dropped to her knees.

Gazing up into his eyes and grasping his cock, she said, "Fuck me, Bishop," then circled her lips around his mushroomed cock head.

Fallan didn't wait to hear him respond, didn't think he'd answer in the negative if the throbbing of his cock on her tongue was anything to go by. She slid him to the back of her throat and sucked him down, drawing up her tongue to swirl around the head, tasting the tiny pearl of his pre-release before bobbing her head back down. He tugged on her hair to stop her but she held firm. As he made to pull her up and off his cock again, she took more of him in her mouth.

She wanted him to release on her tongue, to have the power to make *him* lose control. After a few minutes of her sucking, he managed to draw her off him, taking her arms and tugging her to stand.

"You like sucking my cock, don't you?" he growled seconds before sealing his lips over hers.

Fallan didn't know why he would ask her a question and then not give her the time to answer. She didn't care — she wanted his lips, tongue and cock. Her body was molten heat. She sunk her fingers into his hair then eased back, stopping the toe-curling kiss with reluctance.

"I love sucking cock," she said, staring into his eyes, daring him to refuse her.

She went to go to her knees again, but Bishop held her steady.

"When I want my dick sucked, I'll tell you. Now, explain why you suddenly want me."

Bishop folded his arms and she let out a sigh. Why, when she was willing and ready to do anything he wanted, did he develop the need to understand her actions? God, she just wanted to fuck, to forget. After all she'd been through, she deserved a few hours of pleasure, surely?

"Why don't you shut your mouth and fuck me?" she suggested, not in the mood to argue.

"Call me suspicious."

Glancing round the room, she tried to think of a way to show him what she wanted without him thinking she was working on an ulterior motive. There was no double meaning—she hadn't been looking for anything but money to pay off the debts, a quick holiday and something to take her mind off the worries of the world. Why did he have to think she was after something else?

He stared at her.

Screw it. She didn't have anything to lose and she refused to give up the moment. This whole scenario was a fantasy and one she wanted to see play out to completion.

Ignoring his domineering presence, she sat on the edge of the bath. Staring into his eyes, she opened her legs, disappointed when he didn't move his gaze. He gave no sign that what she was showing him affected him in any way. So not fair, but she would keep going.

"You don't want me?" She placed her hands on the tops of her thighs, sinking her short nails into her flesh, and closed her eyes for a second as the biting contact made her quiver with delight.

"It's not about want," he said.

Fallan chuckled. "That's right, I'd bet to you it's about opportunity. You think I'm someone I'm not. That your rooting around in files, finding out I'm 'just your average woman' means I fit into some mould where I want hearts and flowers, a romantic love affair. Well, you're wrong. I want a fuck, plain and simple. No strings, no recriminations, just sex." She moved her fingers up and down, each time going further towards the inside of her thighs and up, touching the smattering of hair at the apex.

"I'm not about to take a chance," he said. "In my experience, women are liars."

"That's a shame. My pussy is soaking wet for a nice hard cock, and, looking at you, I see yours easily fits the bill." She touched her pussy and let out a whimper. She made sure to keep her gaze on him even though the call of her clit was too strong for her to ignore. "You don't want to touch or taste me?"

Taking her fingers out of her wet heat, she brought her finger to her lips. She would do anything to get what she wanted, to take the upper hand.

"Stop!" Bishop demanded.

Hiding her smile, she got up off her perch and went over to him. Her fingers glistened, and she held them up so he could see how much she wanted him.

"What do you want, big guy?" she asked.

Her acting improving with every second, she licked her lips and tried with all her might not to look at his shaft.

"You think you're winning?" He stared at her, gaze steely.

"Why don't you have a taste and then tell me you don't want me?"

She raised her fingers to his mouth and smeared her cream over his lips. She didn't break eye contact, refusing to give up.

"You have no idea what you're dealing with." Bishop caught her hand then slowly flicked out his tongue, sucking the juice from each finger.

Every pull of his suction further awakened her desire. The final digit-sucking had her ready to pounce on him.

"You taste sweet."

"I'm a sweet girl."

Bishop took her hands and walked her backwards, unlocking the door and manoeuvring her out of the bathroom and through to the bedroom. He forced her to sit on the edge of the bed. She didn't doubt his guidance – she had the feeling Bishop wouldn't hurt her…at least not until they'd fucked.

"I don't think anything about you is sweet," he said.

"Why don't you have more of a taste and make a decision then?" Fallan lay back, spread her legs and stared at him in challenge.

Would he suck her? Or leave her?

In Fallan's eyes, no man was decent unless he was willing to give a woman oral sex. Those she'd been with had always expected head but had never returned the favour.

"You want me to suck your pussy?"

"I want you to do with me whatever the hell you want. Providing you give me an orgasm and a good shag, I'm up for anything." Wasn't that the truth? Fallan felt like a slut – a bad, sexy slut – but, God, this was exciting.

"I'm going straight to hell," he muttered.

"I'm joining you."

He knelt before her and Fallan held her breath as he looked at her. She knew her pussy was attractive. One of her first sexual lessons by a much older lover had taught her to look at herself and to like what she saw.

She could never expect anyone to love her or her body if she didn't love it herself. She'd always enjoyed fingering herself while looking in the mirror. Call it the dirty slut inside her or just a woman truly connected with her mind and body, but it turned her on to see her fingers working over her wet slit.

"You gonna suck me or just stand there?" she asked.

"Soon, baby. I just want to look at you. You've got a nice, red, sweet pussy."

He touched the pubic hair lightly covering her outer lips then opened her, exposing her private parts for his viewing pleasure.

"So small, tight and hot." He inserted a finger then took it out to press it against her hard clit.

Fallan moaned at each sensation.

"Tight."

She revelled in his compliments. He plunged a second finger inside followed by teasing her clit with his tongue. Fallan almost came undone. He pulled her back from the brink of ecstasy by taking his fingers and mouth away.

"Please, let me come," she begged.

"Not until I say so. You're a feisty one." He added a third finger.

"You've only known me a few hours, you don't know the real me," she panted out, gasping as he turned his finger, stroking the sweet spot inside her.

"Yet, in the few hours we've known each other, you've already had my dick in your mouth and your clit in my mouth," he teased.

"Imagine what could happen when we've known each other longer."

Bishop pulled his fingers out and licked them, her pussy already creaming for more of what he had to offer.

"Will you just fuck me already?" she asked, his display making her clit pulse.

"We've got plenty of time."

He returned his tongue to her clit and continued to taste and torture her. She imagined her lips were red and swollen. Her tender clit felt thick and throbbed to the point of pain. Fallan screamed out for any type of release he could give her.

Bishop grasped her by the hips and turned her over. "Get on your knees."

She complied with his order — she'd do anything for him to bring her to orgasm. This guy had strength and stamina and she wanted all of it thrusting inside her cunt.

"You desperate for a pounding, Fallan?"

A jerk of the head was all she could give him. He ran his fingers over her plump arse, gripping her hips and pulling her back into his body. No more teasing, she couldn't stand any more.

"The tops of your thighs are soaking wet, baby. Are you sure you don't want me?"

"I don't want you. I just want your dick."

"Big words for a small woman. Are you sure you can handle me?"

"Fuck me and see."

Fallan couldn't see what he was doing and couldn't wait to find out. She reached between her legs to touch her needy clit.

Bishop slapped her hands away. "My clit to touch."

Moments later, he impaled his cock inside her, the stretch and burn exquisite. Resting her head on her arms, she cried out and succumbed to him bedding her.

"So wet," he murmured.

"Harder!" She moaned, a wrench of noise that didn't sound like it belonged to her.

He withdrew all the way out then lunged back inside, not waiting for her to become accustomed to his size. He took what he wanted, slamming her with relentless force.

Fallan loved it.

Their cries echoed off the walls. She fisted the duvet and pushed back onto him as he thrust up to meet her.

She wanted his cock and everything it had to offer.

"Fuck me harder," she said.

He gave her his all, his hold bruising on her hips, all of his strength and power concentrated in his jabbing thrusts.

Fallan was so close. "Give me release!"

He let go of one hip and touched her swollen jewel, rubbing her to a heart-stopping orgasm within seconds. He wouldn't let up when she started coming, shuddering and crying out with pleasure and satisfaction that she'd got what she wanted.

"You're a wild woman. Fucking tight cunt. I could become addicted to this."

He slapped her arse and pounded away, the main force of her orgasm tightening around him. She imagined her flow of juice glistening on his cock. He still rubbed her, forcing her body into a second orgasm, fiercer and harsher than the first, making her body liquid jelly.

"You have such a pretty arse." He removed his hand from her clit and ran her juice along the crack. "Ever been fucked in the arse?" he asked, shunting into her and fondling her rear hole.

She grunted, not knowing what to say even as the light touch he pressed on her was entirely erotic.

"You're small but I'd fit, fill you nice and full." He pushed a finger inside.

"What are you doing?" she gasped out.

"Testing the waters. You're hot and tight in there."

The sensation wasn't entirely unpleasant but the feelings were more intense and unlike anything she'd felt before.

She wanted him in her arse.

Bishop was turning her into a rutting beast.

"You like that, don't you?" he asked. "Like my finger in your arse and my cock in your cunt."

Fallan shook her head in denial.

"You do, I can feel your cum on my dick. You're wet and hot for it."

As though to prove his point, he eased a second finger inside her arse. Screaming in pleasure her only response, she waited to see what he'd do next.

"You going to let me fuck that arse, Fallan Jones?"

His cock and fingers fucking her together at the same time, in sync with each other, felt like she was being taken by two men, one big and one small.

"I don't know you well enough for that," she said, knowing the excuse was feeble, that he might not believe she was pretending she didn't want it.

"We've known each other a few hours and I'm fucking your cunt, so why not your arse?"

"Wait until we've known each other for longer and I'll see."

But you'd better fuck my arse before this deal is over.

Bishop pounded harder. "I'm going to come."

He pulled his fingers out of her arse and grabbed her hips again, driving into her cunt harder, faster. The tension built until she was screaming out a third orgasm that made her twitch and jolt with its sharp intensity.

Bishop drew her back one final time then growled out his release. Fallan felt it inside her body, the kick of his cock and the explosion of semen, the hot pulse of fluid dripping out of her cunt.

Gasping for breath, she collapsed in a heap with Bishop on top of her, their bodies wet from sweat. He pulled out of her, curving his arm round her waist. Fallan rolled over and snuggled against him, tired but sated.

At least for now.

"You're going to be the death of me, woman."

She smiled, content…

Before all the rushing memories erupted. She was Fallan Jones, an employee for a supermarket. She'd been kidnapped by a man who could kill her.

Out of all of the panic and fear that consumed her in a massive wave, only one point stuck in her mind.

She'd just had unprotected sex with a stranger.

Chapter Five

Bishop waited until Fallan's breathing had evened out and a soft snore left her before he got out of bed. He was reluctant to leave her. Wanted nothing more than to rest beside her, wondering how the hell he'd got so lucky in finding a woman who didn't mind a fuck for fucking's sake. One who didn't go on about commitment before she spread her legs. One who hadn't expected to engage him in a long, drawn-out conversation after she'd been fucked, instead falling asleep like the proverbial man as soon as her head touched his chest. He sounded like an arsehole, he knew that, but the course of his life had made him that way. Self-preservation was a strong thing, gripping him with pincer-like fingers and sending him into a world where emotions didn't exist.

Couldn't exist.

His current situation didn't allow for him to wallow in thoughts of where Fallan had been all his life since...*her*...and what he'd been missing out on from then until now. No, he had shit to sort out, calls to make and, without a doubt, would have Waterman on his arse if he wasn't careful. Still, if the government did their job he'd be safe. They'd made it clear in the past he was one of their best operatives, someone they wouldn't want to do without. His job was safe, providing he toed the line, and seeing as he had nothing left in life *but* his job, he would remain working for them.

He took a quick shower, mindful that the women he'd been involved with in the past—apart from *her*— were a wily set of bitches that wouldn't think twice at feigning sleep and escaping. If Fallan tried it she'd come up short—he'd locked the deadbolts on the doors and hidden the keys, and this place was in the middle of nowhere. Good luck to her finding another human to help her out before her legs gave way from an exhaustive search for help. But he acknowledged he'd be disappointed if he caught her awake and prowling around. She'd already lied about wanting him—and, by God, she'd been a vixen once she'd admitted she needed a fuck—and he wouldn't put it past her to lie again. Even if she was as innocent as she and her files proclaimed, it was human instinct to flee from a situation that was dangerous or one she didn't want to be in.

As he soaped his cock, he thought about whether she was bothered she'd let him take her without protection. She wasn't to know those files he'd accessed also included her medical records and he knew she was clean and receiving the contraceptive injection. Wasn't she worried about venereal disease…or worse? Did her need to be fucked surpass being sensible? Which led him to another thought he didn't much like—she'd possibly weighed her options and decided catching something was a small price to pay if it meant gaining his trust, making him drop his guard so she could get away.

And he'd have let her get away if her life wasn't in danger, albeit with a sense of regret because he'd found a woman who was on the same level as him in the bedroom. Her life *was* in danger, too, he'd be a fool to think otherwise. With Waterman involved in the holiday scam, using Freddie fucking Lash as his man who doled out the threats, she didn't stand a chance. If they got hold of her now she'd disappear for good, just one more unsolved missing persons case the police scratched their heads over.

He stepped out of the shower and dried off, returning to the bedroom with his stomach in knots in case he found the bed empty. Last thing he needed was to deal with her demanding he let her leave, or, worse, seeing her arse hanging out of the window as she scrambled to go home.

Despite his fears, Fallan was still there, hair splayed over the pillow, mouth slightly open, eyes flickering with REM. As relief poured through him, he wondered what she was dreaming about, whether he featured in the scenario going on inside her sleepy head, then chastised himself for being the soft bastard he once was. Why should he suddenly care what she saw? Why did it matter whether he was the star of her night-time imaginings?

He didn't know why he cared but he did. She'd intrigued him in the hotel dining room, intrigued him more with her lies in the bathroom, and well and truly hooked him with her about-face thereafter. He couldn't pinpoint what it was exactly that had gripped him, though. She was nice to look at, no doubt about it, and he liked the way she gave as good as she got while being fucked — loved her greediness in ensuring she got satisfaction—but there was something he couldn't define that drew her to him.

He needed to watch himself. She had the ability to slip under his skin and stay there, a constant itch he needed to scratch if he allowed it. He'd be better off letting his boss, Huntington, take her over, let him keep her safe until this crap was sorted out, but…

He couldn't do it. Huntington would claim her as one of his women, fucking her every which way until he tired of her. She didn't deserve that, even if she did have a healthy sexual appetite. Allowing some hulking government toady to paw her, a pot-bellied, slack-lipped wanker with a penchant for kink, wasn't ideal. Bishop shrugged. Who was he to decide what she did and whom she slept with? For all he knew, now that the promised money may not be forthcoming from Waterman, Fallan might choose to get paid for sex by Huntington. She needed cash, and desperate times called for desperate measures.

Bishop was startled to find his stomach churning at the prospect of her in another man's arms.

What the fuck?

Besides, she couldn't go to Huntington. Bishop wanted to know more about her. Not some shit in a file that told him whether she was a criminal or not. No, he wanted to know about her likes and dislikes, what she enjoyed and what she didn't, and whether her arsehole was as tight around his cock as it had been on his fingers.

She hadn't fooled him with that. Her cunt had spasmed harder when he'd introduced his fingers to her arse. She'd been lying again when she'd made out she'd have to know him better before he breached that hole with his cock. No matter. He'd get to know her better, know her for longer, then he'd see what her excuse would be when he asked her if she'd like his to be the first dick that penetrated her puckered barrier.

What the hell is wrong with you, man?

He rasped a hand over his chin, the sound of stubble somewhat obscene in the virtual silence. Fallan had him at sixes and sevens, acting differently than he had with other women. He didn't usually get so aggressive, didn't usually speak to them as though they were nothing, yet this woman inspired him to do just that. And it didn't seem like she minded either. From what he'd gathered so far, she was open to a bit of filthy talk, a bit of ordering about. A bit of degradation.

She suited him down to the ground.

Fuck.

He turned from her, cock stirring once again, and checked the window locks. After the imagery of her naked arse going out of an open window, he needed to be sure the place was secure. He didn't want her leaving...and not just because of her safety, either.

It was a bitter pill to swallow, knowing a woman had affected him like this again. He'd always been in control in the past, had always known one-night stands were the way to go since —

He wasn't going to think about the past, damn it!

Bishop slipped on a pair of jeans then headed for the living room, forcing Fallan from his thoughts with great difficulty. The sight of the phone on his desk helped erase her, though. He had a report call to make — one that would have his boss in a thunderous temper if his previous reactions to shit like this were any indication. He dialled and waited for Huntington to pick up, pulled out of either a call girl or an alcohol-induced sleep. His boss liked the whisky and wasn't averse to sinking a fair few before he retired at night.

"What do you want?" Huntington asked, going on with, "I saw you'd accessed the files. What woman are you fucking now when you're supposed to be working?"

"I picked her up at the drop zone." Bishop staved off a wave of irritation that threatened to consume him. Huntington was a prick who never failed to get on his last nerve.

"And you disturbed me to tell me something that could wait until morning? Or are you bored while you keep watch on her as she sleeps?"

"It couldn't wait until morning, and I'm not watching her. She's sleeping but the house is secure, as it always is."

Huntington sighed, and Bishop imagined it was tainted by the scent of stale alcohol, pitied any woman his phone call had also awakened if she got a blast of his breath. He shivered and waited for a response.

"So what is it?" It sounded as though Huntington was sitting himself up.

"Waterman's involved."

"Fuck."

"Indeed."

"How so?" Huntington was fully alert now. His voice had lost that weary, condescending edge.

"He's the one in charge of the drops. How he came by the information is anyone's guess, but it's him using blackmail to make those in the government bow down to him. He set up some elaborate scam, would you believe?"

"Yes, I do believe, which is why we sent our own men, you included, to intercept the packages. Go on."

"He had the microchips with evidence of government foul play on them—it was him or one of his men who contacted someone in government about their existence. According to Miss Jones, he made up a competition, ensuring women won a short holiday break, and their instructions were to deliver the chips in velvet pouches to specific locations in each hotel. We knew someone was doing that, didn't we? Just not him. After Miss Jones secreted the cargo—and she was promised thousands of pounds once she'd completed her task—I intercepted, as planned. Waterman sent another of his goons to collect—a double-cross, I assume. He probably intended to make out he knew nothing of it once news of the pick-up going wrong had come to light. We anticipated this. And I was seen taking the goods."

"Wonderful. Do continue."

"I had to take the female to my present location as I thought she may have been with Waterman, but it appears she's innocent."

"I saw her file myself and would be inclined to agree, but even files can be deceptive. Tampered with. What's her reaction been like?"

Bishop thought of her reaction—but not the initial one Huntington meant. He tossed the image of her sitting on the bath edge with her legs open from his mind and rewound to see fury and incomprehension on her face when he'd approached her outside the hotel. "She's either innocent or a bloody good actress."

"Anything else?"

"I was followed from the hotel. Probably the man Waterman sent to collect."

"Marvellous." The word was full of disgust and sarcasm.

"I gave him the slip, but it won't be long before they're on the lookout for my licence plate."

"They haven't spotted it since you infiltrated his mob, so why the devil would they find you via your vehicle now?"

"I suppose…"

"New plates will solve it. Should have done that before. Bloody got sidetracked with other things."

"Yes." *Like shoving your cock into women.*

Bishop waited for further instruction. Huntington didn't seem in a hurry to offer any—he did that often, just left the line open while he thought things out, leaving Bishop hanging on until he deigned to speak. While he listened to what he imagined was Huntington getting out of bed and walking downstairs to his alcohol cabinet—a nasty, tacky-looking globe where the top half opened to reveal even tackier crystal decanters—Bishop glanced at the monitors on a shelf above his desk. His cameras were trained on all areas of his property. The grounds were in darkness, nothing untoward going on, and he let out a breath of relief. He wasn't afraid of what he'd have to do if someone did happen by—he was trained in armed combat and had no conscience with regard to sinking a bullet or knife into anyone who threatened to expose him or the government officials he was contracted with—but he had Fallan to consider now. She hadn't seen a gun let alone handled one until she'd met him, and false bravado wasn't enough to get her out of a tricky situation.

This location had been secure for years. It didn't exist as far as any regular Joe was concerned. It wasn't on any files other than governmental ones, and he didn't receive any mail or deliveries. He picked up his post from a PO box and bought whatever he needed himself. His credit cards were at his other, civilian address, and the name on them was a far cry from any he'd used while working. He rarely went 'home', though. That place contained too many memories, too much of his past that he'd forced himself to forget.

After... Well, years ago, when...when things had gone wrong, he'd removed all photographs of... Removed things that reminded him of what he'd lost, what his job had made him lose, and vowed never to dwell on them again. Every so often *she* infiltrated his thoughts, but he quelled them, pushed the sight of her smiling face away because seeing her made him hurt.

He clenched his teeth, annoyed that he'd let her in again, if only for the briefest of moments. He'd failed her, put her in danger, and she hadn't even been aware of it until it had been too late.

Until the bullet had ripped off the side of her face and ricocheted through her brain, taking her away from him. From that traumatic, absolutely hateful day, he'd vowed never to allow a woman into his life again. Never to let a woman be in the danger she had been in.

You can't even bear to think of her name, can you?

No, he couldn't. And wouldn't. Ever.

Guilt rested heavily on his shoulders, a burden he'd carry to the grave. He worked twenty-four/seven, burying himself in his jobs so he didn't have a second to pause and think. And now here he was, allowing another woman to get to him, making him want to know her in ways he shouldn't. Was he ready to try again, was that it? Had years of one-night stands and abstinence in between trysts given him enough time to grieve? To forget? To forgive himself?

I'll never forgive my fucking self.

"Uh, there's been a development," Huntington said, his razor-sharp tone hauling Bishop out of his thoughts and into the present.

"What is it?" Bishop's heart rate increased, the familiarity of adrenaline surging through his veins erasing the last vestiges of thoughts from the past.

"Seems someone—Waterman's crew, I suspect—has enlisted the *help*, shall we say, of a CCTV camera operator in the city. They've been for a little visit. Frankie Lash, to be precise."

"Fuck." Bishop hiked in a long breath, then let it out slowly. "I know what you're going to say."

"You do? So what's your next course of action?"

"Get the fuck out of here before they work out where my vehicle could have headed after it was last captured on camera."

"Good lad. The next location—you know the drill."

"I do."

"And take Miss Jones with you, blindfolded, of course."

"Of course." Bishop paused then asked, "The CCTV operator?"

"He has a new, bigger smile, so I'm told."

"Shit."

"He's on his way to hospital. I'm sure they'll stitch his cheeks up and send him on his way in no time. Whether he's left alone after that isn't our concern."

"What? Are you shitting me? You're going to let him go back to his usual life knowing Waterman and his wankers will go after him again?"

"We can't take care of every casualty, Bishop."

Bishop bit back a snide retort. He worked for a government where he always put himself in danger for its MPs, this time to prevent some sordid, sexual information being leaked to the press. He worked on behalf of men and women who weren't prepared to make sure those who had been hurt when Bishop did his job—innocent civilians just going about their lives—were cared for in the event things went tits up. People drawn into messes they didn't know they were in until it hit them in the face—messes created by the very MPs who professed to care for their constituents when they went live on TV while touring the country for their campaigns.

The whole lot of them made Bishop sick, and he came to the sudden realisation he wanted out.

"This is my last job," he said, then gritted his teeth.

"I don't think so," Huntington said. "It's so very easy for us to plant information. You know that as well as I do."

And it's so easy for me to gain a new identity and fuck off.

Huntington cleared his throat. "Stop being so dramatic and get on with it. By the sounds of things, it won't be long before Waterman comes knocking on your door."

Chapter Six

Waterman drummed his fingers on his desk blotter. "Sounds like a plan."

"You coming with us?" Frankie asked, his expression showing hope, like some constantly kicked puppy wishing that just this once he'd be petted.

"I think I will, seeing as it's that wanker we're dealing with. I'd love to know what name he's using for this job. Bet it's something he'll be dying to tell me when I have his nuts in a vice and he realises there's no way out."

Frankie laughed. "Nice one, boss."

Waterman stifled a sigh. Frankie really was getting on his nerves lately, almost as much as Kemp, who stood in front of his desk, face like a slapped arse. Waterman guessed Kemp was pissed off at Frankie pipping him to the post. What Kemp had to suck up was that Waterman gave the orders. Frankie had been sent to deal with the CCTV man, and Kemp was supposed to be finding out where that wanker might have gone. And by that instruction he'd meant for

Kemp to visit the hotel and ask a few questions. Instead, Kemp had driven out of the city, parked on a quiet side street, and let a prozzer entertain him until Waterman had given him a call to say Frankie had come up with the goods.

He'd deal with Kemp later.

Waterman would never forget that wanker's name. Rook, it was, Peter Rook, but if he worked for the government, as Waterman had found out, he wouldn't be using the same name now. But he'd be finding out what his alias was very shortly when they turned up at his hideout and forced it out of him.

Would Rook bleat, though, that was the question. A man contracted to work for the government wasn't known for caving during torture. Rook would keep all the information to himself, of that Waterman had no doubt. Still, what did a name matter, anyway? Slicing off his bollocks and feeding them to the fishes was all he needed to make him feel better. Rook being introduced to the Thames would be satisfaction enough for Rook gaining his trust the way he had when he'd worked for him. Mind you, a bit of torture passed the time, didn't it? Gave them all a laugh, a bit of a breather, so toying with Rook before they offed him was definitely on the cards.

"Right, you have his location, you say?" Waterman asked Frankie, deliberately keeping Kemp out of the conversation.

"Yep. Our CCTV man worked out Rook lives in some remote farmhouse in the sticks. Fifteen or so miles away, give or take."

"Right." Waterman picked up a half-smoked cigar from his ashtray and used it to crush the ash in the bottom. "And our CCTV bloke—how was he after he gave that information?"

Frankie stuck out his chest, prancing from foot to foot as though in the corner of a boxing ring, more than ready to start the next round. "Reckoned he wouldn't do anything like that for us again. Went on about him losing his job if he did. Same shite as last time."

"And how did you respond?" Waterman had a damn good idea, but he liked hearing his employees relate their actions all the same.

"Gave him a Cheshire cat, didn't I?" Frankie nodded a few times, still prancing.

"Nice one. He knows we mean business. He'll be in my employ now, I think." Waterman lit his cigar, holding the smoke in his mouth before blowing out smoke rings.

"Yeah, I told him he might be," Frankie said, finally halting his irritating dance.

"And you, Kemp." Waterman stared at him, leaning back in his chair to take another puff of his cigar. "What did you come up with?"

"I didn't find anything out," he said, trying and failing to keep his eyes from darting left to right.

"Ah, well. Doesn't matter," Waterman said jovially. *It does – oh, it fucking does, you tosser.* "So long as we got the result we wanted. Right. Frankie, get on the blower and tell what's-his-name to get the car ready. Kemp...you sit your arse down here and have a nice drink with me while we wait."

Although it was the middle of the night, Waterman wasn't affected by being out at such an hour. Most of his work was done in the darkness, his body clock set to him kipping during the day and coming alive in the evening. Daylight had a habit of showing up all the starkness of blood, the colour so much more startling when the sun shone. Had a habit of alerting the good citizens of London that something was amiss. A man stabbed in broad daylight while out shopping with his missus. A bloke mowed down by a bus as he crossed the road on his way to the local boozer. Although some jobs had to be done in daylight hours, he preferred the majority of them to be completed in the shadows. Less chance of witnesses. Better chance of getting away with it.

He sat in the back of the car, What's-his-name driving them to their location, the man unaware of why they were going, and not enquiring why, either. He was a good sort. Did his job, looked the other way, and, as far as Waterman was aware, kept his mouth shut. Frankie and Kemp sat opposite, Frankie looking pleased with himself for a job well done and Kemp appearing decidedly queasy. Waterman had plied the latter with brandy and a tab of LSD — two large shots that had Kemp wincing as Waterman encouraged him to drink up quick — and Kemp had eyed him oddly, no doubt sensing the tension that had sprung between them once Frankie had left the room.

Fucking tosser ought to know me better by now. I carry no one, let no one take the piss out of me.

"You all right there, Kemp?" he asked, keeping a poker face. "Only, you appear to be a bit peaky."

"I'm fine thanks, Guv," Kemp said, staring out of the window at the countryside spilling by, eyes glazed, fingers twitching on his knees.

Waterman followed suit. No street lamps here, only the glow of the moon, its meagre illumination doing nothing but giving the world a dark grey hue where it touched, the rest in black shadow. Trees zoomed past, stout, spiky branches stabbing the air, twigs on the ends resembling hands in star shapes or giving a two-fingered salute. Clouds scudded across the moon, swift on their journey, indicating quite a breeze must have picked up since they'd got in the car.

Bored of the scenery, Waterman returned his attention to the interior of the car. He opened his mouth to make small talk, but the glass partition between the rear and What's-his-name in the front hummed down.

"We're almost there, Guv," the driver said. "Place over there to your right, look."

Waterman did look, spying a squat dwelling that sat in a field all by itself. No trees, no coverage. Dangerous.

"Cheers," he said, reminding himself to become reacquainted with the driver's name once they got back to his office.

The car turned right and What's-his-name slowed as he drove them up what felt beneath the tyres to be an asphalt track. He doused the headlights, and Waterman leant forward to get a better glimpse of the place out of the windshield. From the shape of it the building was a non-descript farmhouse, something no one would take any notice of if they drove past. The lack of anything around it was a wise move on Rook's—or the government's—part. Rook would be able to see in all directions, his sights clear to the fields beyond, to the sides, and the road ahead.

They drew closer, and Waterman's stomach knotted. He hadn't been out on a job in a long while—getting on in years had seen to that—but it didn't mean he wasn't able to look after himself in a dodgy scenario. He kept fit pumping iron, jogged once or twice a week, a minder at his heels, and indulged in target practice—not that he could ever forget how to use a gun. Didn't hurt to pop a few shots off every now and again, though, did it?

The car came to a halt, and Waterman nodded at Frankie and Kemp. They got out and disappeared into the darkness, coming back after a few minutes to proclaim the outside was clear. No traps, no men hiding around corners. Waterman got out, adrenaline spiking.

He rapped on the driver's window and waited for it to glide down. "Turn around, mate, and wait for us."

Waterman strode towards the Cotswold stone house, narrowing his eyes at the windows. No bars, but he'd bet his last quid that was toughened glass— bulletproof, most likely. The front door looked like any other, except, if Rook was as savvy as Waterman suspected, it would be lined with steel, the opaque glass panels as bulletproof as the windows. He nodded, impressed at how normal the place seemed, when, in fact, it could be riddled with booby traps with Rook lying in wait inside. He lifted one hand and flicked his wrist.

Frankie was the first to obey the silent command. He went to the car boot, now facing the house, and popped the lock. He brought out a battering ram, over a metre long, in daylight a lurid yellow but in this light a murky grey. Waterman nodded, and Frankie went to work. The door was a stubborn bastard but opened eventually, swinging back on its hinges and smacking against the interior wall with an almighty crash. The noise was nothing compared to that which the ram had made, and it was a good job the location had no neighbours otherwise Waterman would have had more people to silence.

Frankie went inside, but Kemp remained on the doorstep, teetering a bit. The cold fresh air had probably made him feel drunker and more out of sorts than he had when getting in the car.

Waterman grinned. "Don't fancy doing a search-and-find then, Kemp?"

Kemp shook his head. "No," he said, the word sounding like *nose*. "You don't employ me for that kind of thing. I don't even know why you 'sisted on bringing me here."

Being even bolder now he's having a trip, is he? Cheeky bastard.

"Thought you might like to see how things are done on this side of it," Waterman said. "I mean, it's all very well being the one who goes around quietly finding out information, but I feel it's best to know all aspects of the business, wouldn't you agree?"

"Nose," Kemp said, nodding to a beat only he could hear.

Frankie appeared in the doorway, his face grim, eyes blazing.

"Well?" Waterman asked.

Frankie shook his head. "No one here, boss."

"Any sign they have been?" Waterman frowned at Kemp, who wove through imaginary obstacles, arms out in front as though he was wading through foliage.

Prick.

"Yep, bed's still warm." Frankie bit his bottom lip and clenched his hands.

"Just missed him, then." Waterman sighed and stared at Kemp again. "Still, seems a shame to waste such a quiet location." He smiled at Frankie.

"What d'you mean, boss?"

"Well, there's no one around to hear any screams, is there?" Waterman jerked his head in Kemp's direction.

Frankie nodded and approached the tottering man. Waterman turned and walked to the car, getting in the back seat, pleased by the warmth.

"Give those two a minute," he said to What's-his-name. "Then Frankie will be out and we'll get back to the office."

Chapter Seven

Fallan couldn't see a thing. Bishop said it was better this way, if she didn't know where he was taking her, but the blindfold chafed the bridge of her nose, making her want to rip it off.

Not the best way to wake up but she supposed it was better than looking at the business end of a loaded gun. The whole secrecy thing was beginning to annoy her, though.

"Is this really necessary?" she asked for the umpteenth time.

"I've told you it is."

She growled in frustration and moved her hands together, the metal of cuffs chaffing her wrists. Life was so unfair at times.

"Just out of curiosity, will I be home in time to pay the ten grand off on my house?" she asked, wondering if she'd even get it now.

"We had sex last night and you want to know about paying your debt? I rather thought the sex would have been at the forefront of your mind."

Fallan smiled. He sounded a little insecure.

"What can I say? I'm not the type of girl to remember one-night stands."

The van took a swerve and her arm connected with the side panel where she sat in the back. "Ouch. Either drive carefully or budge over and let me drive." She couldn't even rub the sore spot. Damn cuffs.

"Stop ordering me around. I'm the one who calls the shots."

"Is this really necessary with the cuffs?" She thrust her wrists in the direction she guessed Bishop was driving.

He sighed. "How many times have I told you? Yes, they are."

"You know, you were fucking me not long ago and all of a sudden I'm treated like the most wanted criminal in London. How many times must I tell *you* that all I want to do is pay off my house and deal with the fact my mum died and my life is shit?" She screamed the last bit, her anger coming forward.

If she could have lashed out and smacked him she would have done.

"I thought you didn't mind fucking," Bishop said.

"Oh, that is just bloody great, that is—you thinking of the sex first. Typical man. I've got more problems than a little shag, Bishop. I've got to deal with my house, my life, and work. It may be easy for you with your whole secret life and messed-up career with no money issues, but to those of us who have a *normal* job with *normal* pay, it's important to keep it. If I don't get back home by tomorrow, I won't have a job on Monday when I'm supposed to be back there. Not only will you and your cock keep me out of a job, but they'll make me lose my house, and to add to that I'll probably end up at the bottom of some dirty, disgusting river because you'll kill me. So no, this is not about the fucking for me."

Fallan slammed her hands on her knees and turned to what she hoped were the rear doors. She didn't want to talk to him anymore. Her heart raced with the anger surging through her. Out of all the problems she could have, Bishop — or sex with him — wasn't one of them. Well, *he* was a problem because he was currently taking her God knew where for God knew what reason. She hadn't been lying when she'd said she thought she'd end up at the bottom of some dirt-infested water. Having unprotected sex with him hardly came into it because of that.

"Are you done?" he asked.

"Would it matter if I'm not?"

"I was expecting some hysterical woman cursing and having a go at me, not worrying about all the other problems," he said.

"I'm a normal girl with normal problems and I want nothing to do with the shit that goes on with what you're dealing with. Now, please tell me, will I be able to pay the money on my house?"

The house she'd grown up in and the one place she loved more than anything. Her parents had taken out a second mortgage and used the money to help with medical bills. They'd opted to go private. The NHS queue had been too damn long for them to get treated quickly. They'd had her quite late in life, and by the time she'd been ready to go out and enjoy the world she'd been dealing with two sick parents. Having anonymous sex with strangers had been the easiest way to seek the release she needed at the end of a hard and stressful day. But being with Bishop last night had been the first time she hadn't used any protection, and now she wished she had, just in case he *did* take her home at some point. Since her mother died, she'd vowed to find that special someone to spend her life with. Her mother had asked as her dying wish for her to find someone she would love for the rest of her life and who she could spend good, quality time with. Fallan hadn't wanted to burst her mother's bubble by saying she doubted any man like that existed for her, so she'd agreed. The problem was, after dealing with her death and everything that went with it, Fallan couldn't remember if she was up to date on her contraceptive jabs.

The waste-of-time anonymous sex had stopped and with it the need to get the shot.

Shit. But hey, that feeling of me eventually ending up in the river just won't go away, so what the hell? Whole life's been a mess so why ever expect anything less? Things getting worse is the order of how it's always been. Fuck it.

Bishop cleared his throat. "I don't know if you'll be back in time to pay the money. I don't know if they'll even pay you the money because I have the package they asked you to deliver."

"Oh, this is just fucking *great!*" Her heart stuttered. She felt sick. Shivers took over her body. *What the hell am I going to do now?*

"We're here," he said.

"Does that mean I can take the blindfold off?"

"Not yet."

Fallan listened as he pulled to a stop. There were no distinct sounds to give away where they were. She heard him lift the break handle, switch off the lights and turn off the ignition.

"When I get you out I need to know if you're going to try something stupid," he said.

"You mean besides having sex with a complete stranger I know nothing about?" she asked.

"You wanted it as much as I did, so don't try to play the victim."

"Wouldn't dream of it, but I'm not the one who tied you up and put you in a car or van. Anyone ever tell you you're not very trusting?"

"You're not the only one who's told me. Now, are you going to try anything?"

Fallan sat back against the side panel and wondered where they could be for him to need confirmation she wasn't going to try anything. Were there likely to be people about? People in houses who would hear her scream? "When will you let me go?"

"I've told you, I can't tell you that because I don't know."

"Will you ever let me go?"

A pause. Fallan waited. The silence stretched on.

"Okay," she said. "Seeing as you don't want to answer a simple question, maybe you can answer another one that isn't so difficult. Do you intend to kill me?"

This question she really wanted to know the answer to. Her life was in danger and he was the person either putting her in that danger or, as he'd implied, taking her away from it and keeping her safe.

"Please," she said. "For fuck's sake, imagine yourself in my position. If you were me, wouldn't you want to know if you were going to die? Whether you would ever see your home again? Whether you'd get the chance to live because all of a damn sudden you've realised, after being kidnapped and fucked by a stranger, you've been living a shitty, boring life that makes you now want to live a more exciting one?"

Bishop sighed. "I've no intention of killing you. But other people may want to if what you've told me about this holiday weekend shit is true."

Fallan took a deep breath. "Well, I guess you'd better take a chance on me, because I'm not into lying, especially in this kind of situation. If I have people looking for me, like that Freddie or Frankie, or whatever the fuck his name is, I need you to sort them out so I can find some other way to stall the bank on foreclosing." She paused for a few seconds. "Because, if you've got the package, they're not exactly going to be handing me that money now, are they!"

God, she was so angry, so bewildered, so fucking scared all at the same time. What a goddamn mess!

She heard the door open, then slam and the unmistakable sound of gravel as he moved round the vehicle to the back. He climbed in and grasped her knees—turning her to face him? She didn't know. Couldn't fucking *see!*

"I'm going to unlock the cuffs," he said. "*Don't* try anything."

Fallan sat and waited, although she wanted to lash out, and Bishop was the best choice, the only choice to lash out at. She resisted—what good would it do?— and he guided her out. She heard him shut and lock the door, then he cupped her shoulder.

At his touch, all the anger she felt at her situation rushed through her. She pulled out of his grip, not to run but to turn to him and blindly smack out. She didn't know how she managed to strike him but she did, and the slap to his face stung her hand. She bunched her hands and started hitting out at him— every part of his body she could slap and kick, she did.

"You little bitch," he growled, hauling her to him, her blindfold slipping down in the process.

Fallan hesitated, letting her eyes adjust to the early morning glow of the sun. A shithole of a building stood to their right. The place looked as if it was about to fall down. The roof slate bowed in the middle, and the brickwork was mouldy and grey. The front door, aged and weathered, didn't give her confidence that it would keep intruders out. All the front windows were covered in grime except one, which had a clean circle in the centre, made by someone's sleeve cuff or a cloth, she imagined. All in all, things were going from worse to worse.

Abruptly, Bishop lifted her over his shoulder and carried her along a gravel path leading to the cottage, scrubby grass bordering the walkway.

"You bastard! You're going to kill me in there, aren't you?"

She thumped his back and jabbed her knees, connecting with his smooth stomach. He let out a grunt but didn't stop in his mission to get to the cottage.

Fallan didn't give up and continued her beating, even though her fists connected with hard, muscled flesh and yet her thumps didn't appear to affect him.

"Put me down!" she yelled, suddenly and startlingly aware that no one was coming and no one would care if she died.

He ignored her, opened the door and carried her over the threshold. Fallan held still, otherwise she'd have smacked her head on the lintel.

The dust hit her first and she sneezed. She lifted her head to look around. Cobwebs hung from the hallway corners. Plasterwork near the ceiling was cracked, missing in places. The air smelt musty, like a disused library. Bishop closed the door then locked it, putting the key in his pocket. He let her go and she flopped down, knowing she'd allow him to take her where he wanted. Maybe where no spiders would walk over her body.

"I thought this place would shut you up." He chuckled.

Behind him, Fallan squeezed his buttocks — hard — and punched his arse, hoping it hurt but knowing it wouldn't. "Shut your face."

He led her into a panelled room that she assumed would have been a living room at one time. Dust coated the intricate wooden squares surrounding each wall panel as well as the floor — uncarpeted, harboured tufts of rust-coloured pile in the corners and a smattering of loose concrete. Whoever had lived here before hadn't hired a cleaner when they'd vacated, that was for sure. Bishop guided her to the far left corner and kicked a panel. Dust from the wooden surround drifted down and landed on the toe of his boot. A section of wall slid to the right, an ancient creaking sound filling the room, and she stared at a lift door.

About to ask what the fucking hell was going on, Fallen closed her mouth again as the lift door opened. He led her inside the clean interior then jabbed a button. A neon green triangle lit up, indicating that they were going down.

"Who the hell are you?" she asked as the lift stopped, the door opening to a trendy basement-turned-apartment area.

"The only people who come out here are drug dealers and squatters and they're never allowed to stay long enough to catch on to what's below the cottage."

"What happens if someone tries to buy this place up?" Fallan walked to a cream leather sofa, amazed at the contrast between the filth upstairs and the cleanliness down here. Above a mahogany bar in the corner, stocked with enough alcohol for a grand old party, an array of small monitors dotted the wall. Security camera screens?

"Ghost rumours and the general crap appearance keeps potential buyers far away. Not many people travel out here, and, if they did and they spotted this place from the road, no one in their right mind would even want to buy it. It looks like a puff of wind would knock it down. Who the fuck would want to buy a gaff like that? Now, about that punch…"

Bishop thrust her against the wall and pushed her hands above her head. "What am I going to do with you?"

Oddly, she wasn't afraid but she *was* aroused. He did things to her insides he had no business doing. He leaned into her, his cock pressing into her stomach.

"I don't know what you're going to do with me, do I? I'm a woman whose life is in danger, and I'm stuck with a man who thinks I'm some bimbo who'll have sex with him whenever he wants it because he thinks that bimbo will use it as a means of escape. What he doesn't realise, even though I made it clear last time, is that I'll fuck him because I want to fuck him and for no other reason…except maybe it passes the time, makes me feel better, takes me out of the situation I'm in and into another." She'd tried to tease, make light of it, but her pulse pounded, maybe with a little fear, and, damn it, wet heat from her pussy soaked through her panties.

"Nice try at fooling me, but any other woman would try and escape. You've done neither, so try again in convincing me why you seem content to just do as you're told."

"I don't have much choice, do I? I mean, I'm cuffed, I was blindfolded. I supposedly have others looking for me. Dangerous others. You seem the best of a bad lot." Fallan didn't know what else to say so wiggled her hips and undulated. "I was angry and I don't know what came over me when I struck you, but I'm not sorry." As explanations went, it was so close to the truth.

"I should put you over my knee and spank this fine arse you've got."

He released her hands to cup her arse cheeks. Fallan hung her arms around his neck and took his lips in a kiss. Her arousal came fast and hot. She wanted his lips on her body, her cunt.

She thrust her tongue into his mouth, tasting the mint of chewing gum and the essence of who he was. She moaned and pulled back. "You can punish me any way you want for those punches."

No man had dared to smack her arse but if he wanted to put her over his knee then she wouldn't argue. She rather looked forward to feeling the sting of his palm on her backside.

"Is that what you want? For me to strip you naked, put you over my knee and smack this arse until it's red and stinging?"

"Why not? You wanted to fuck it earlier and we've known each other longer than a few hours now," she teased.

He eased his hands under her dress and ran a finger along the line of her panties. "You're wet."

She stared at him, toying with the hair at his nape.

"We've got to stop doing this," he said, kissing her long and deep then rearing back.

"Why? We're both having fun. We have nothing better to do, unless you have something else in mind."

Bishop growled and, picking her up, took her into the centre of the room. Fallan giggled, enjoying the feeling of being held by a strong man.

"You've got some great muscles on you," she said, taking her bound arms from around his neck.

"Don't move," he said.

Fallan was too excited to even think about moving. She wanted to be fucked by him again, her pussy already dripping enough cream that he could slide into her without any trouble. He moved to a metal panel on the wall beside the bar and pressed a button. Music came to life in the large space, a sensual, slow but deeply erotic tune. Bishop got himself seated in front of her in a comfy leather chair.

"I want you to remove your clothes," he said.

"I'm cuffed."

He quickly rose and freed her wrists, putting the cuffs and the key into his jeans pocket.

"I want you to strip for me, but slowly and while dancing," he said.

"You want me to striptease?"

"Yes. Unless you have any objections? I think it's what you owe me for keeping you safe."

Fallan didn't have any objections. Once, when she'd been alone in front of a mirror, she'd danced, swaying her hips from side to side, undressing until she'd stood naked. The experience had teased and delighted her, giving her what had been one of the biggest orgasms of her life…before Bishop.

Smiling, she closed her eyes, allowing the soft beat of the music to flow through her. The rhythm worked and she moved her hips with every erotic beat. She licked her lips and forced herself to open her eyes and stare at him as she slowly pulled down her dress, revealing her simple, white, sheer lace bra that pushed her breasts up but covered her nipples. She turned, giving him her back, and took the dress off, twisting this way and that, her body pulsing and in time with the music. With a sweet smile she went to her knees and crawled towards him, maintaining eye contact with him.

Placing her hands on his knees, she brought herself up, rubbing her bra-covered breasts over the fabric of his jeans. She stood, opened her legs and sat on him, rubbing her wet panties over his bulging crotch, thrusting her breasts into his face.

"What are you doing? I asked for a slow dance," he said, cupping her arse.

"The dance isn't over yet. And I believe the man watching should get a little fun in the process, don't you?"

Fallan kissed him then drew his head into the valley of her breasts. His stubble marked her, making lusty heat shoot to her clit. He moved his hands from her arse to her back and pressed his face harder against her. She continued her torment with her hips, cunt grinding over his hard cock. She wanted to unzip his jeans, ease it out and fuck him, but the teasing turned her on so she continued to gyrate.

"You're making me want you," he said.

"That's the idea."

Fallan reached behind and unclasped her bra, allowing it to fall down her arms. She presented a nipple to his lips and he drew it inside his mouth. She let her head fall back and gasped in pleasure.

He sucked her other nipple, tugging, swirling his tongue around it until Fallan felt she was losing control. She jumped off his lap and resumed dancing, removing her panties then going to her knees again, showing him her exposed pussy.

Her inner thighs were covered in the wet result of her arousal and he stared at her cunt, at the no doubt puffy red lips of her slit.

"Come here," he ordered.

She crawled to him but instead of sitting on his lap she laid herself over his knee.

"I've been a very naughty girl," she said. Fallan didn't know why she played these games with him. With Bishop she wanted to do everything to please him and if it meant giving him her body and mind she'd do that.

"Fucking hell." He caressed her arse cheeks then lifted his hand and delivered a swift swipe. She cried out but the pulse of heat and short, sharp sting had her squeezing her legs together to gain some friction on her clit. She needed contact on her cunt.

His smacks rained down, giving her continued pleasure, and she cried out again—not in pain but from the intense satisfaction.

By the time the last hit landed they were both sweating and panting for breath.

"That felt so good."

She moaned as he gently pushed her to the floor then stood. Through her erotic haze she watched him remove his clothes. His cock, strong and hard, pushed out in front of him and in seconds he was naked.

Bishop grasped her hair and brought his cock to her lips. "Suck it," he demanded.

Fallan opened her mouth and took him inside, tasting pre-cum from his slit. Using her hair as leverage, he fucked her mouth.

"Fucking wicked mouth," he growled.

Fallan cupped his balls, wanting to give him enjoyment. This was more than a one-night stand now. She wanted this. Him. His hard commands and the bliss he could give. Her arse stung from the punishment but she relished it.

She looked up to see Bishop watching her take his cock.

Soon, though, he pulled her off him and sat back down.

"I want you to crawl to me and take my dick in your cunt. I want to watch as you sink down on me." He fingered his bollocks.

Fallan crawled to him, licked her lips, turned on as Bishop fucked his fist, his shaft glistening from her saliva. He was large, fitting her mouth and cunt nicely, and she wanted more of it. She stood and opened her legs, repeating everything she'd done before, only now, as she perched on him, she took his cock and brought it to her entrance. She rubbed him over her clit, coating him in her essence, then lodged him inside her. With her hands on his shoulders, she slowly eased down. She gasped—he did nothing but watch her sink on him.

After she was seated, his balls resting near her arse, she felt full to the top.

"Now ride me," he said.

Fallan did as he'd instructed. They gasped, kissed and panted as he held her hips and pushed her down at the same time he thrust up to meet her. Her breasts bounced with each swift fuck, his strength surprising her. He lifted her off his cock until the head remained inside, then, with one hard slam, he jammed her all the way back onto him. She screamed as he hit the spot deep inside her, so close to pain but delightful all the same, immense pleasure taking over.

"I'm not going to last," he said. "Play with yourself. Touch your cunt. Rub your wet clit. Make yourself come."

She fingered her clit. Bishop took control and sped up her movements. Her clit was hot, on fire, and it only took a few strokes and she was screaming out her release. Her cunt tightened, pulsed hard. A couple more jerks and he shot his own release.

They collapsed. He circled his arms around her. For the second time in years, she felt warm, safe and happy, and she didn't want the feeling to end.

Chapter Eight

Bishop left Fallan to shower alone. She was getting to him, under his damn skin, into his emotions, and he didn't like it, didn't bloody need it. If he allowed himself to get attached he risked making mistakes he couldn't afford. They were safe — for now — but they couldn't stay here indefinitely. She needed to return to her normal life, and at some point before that he'd have to go out and leave her here. Do some undercover work to see what Waterman and his men were up to, ask around discreetly to find out whether they had a bead on where he'd taken her. They'd discovered his other place easily enough, and however they'd done that could be applied to this place and they'd swoop on them. Mind you, all they'd find was a dilapidated cottage, nothing to write home about.

Unless they discovered the wall panel.

Fallan was singing, her soft voice drifting out to him, garbled by shower water. He paced the living area. He'd better contact Huntington and let him know they were secure for now. Maybe his boss would have some new information for him.

In a small office off the living room, he used the regular phone to contact Huntington. Video calling on the laptop wasn't an option, what with Bishop being stark naked. Huntington didn't need to know that his suspicions about Bishop fucking Fallan were correct. He sat on the chair behind the desk and dialled.

"Yes, Bishop?" Huntington said upon answering.

"We're safe at house two."

"I gathered that when the security alarm here bleeped and I saw you and the woman enter. I see the place is still as nasty as ever. Miss Jones, however, is another sight altogether. Although I didn't much enjoy seeing you in the frame in the apartment, watching her fuck you passed some time pleasantly."

Shit. He'd forgotten to switch off the cameras in the basement.

"Silly mistake, don't you think, Bishop?"

"Yes, sir."

"Has she got to you so much that you forgot every movement made in that place is filmed? You know this—it's how we find out someone has broken into the property when none of our agents are in residence—so I can only assume she's so alluring that security measures slipped your mind."

Bishop blushed, annoyed with himself and Huntington, his smug tone grating on Bishop's nerves. "I fucked up. I gave you a show. You probably wanked off while watching. Big deal. I'll turn the cameras off next time."

"Is it wise for there to *be* a next time? Having feelings for her isn't a good idea."

"I don't have feelings for her. She's a job, nothing more."

A soft growl came from behind him, and Bishop turned to the doorway and caught sight of Fallan as she strode naked across the living room and flopped onto the sofa, narrowing her eyes at him. Christ, she was a wildcat. She'd told him she liked to fuck for fucking's sake, yet there she was, eyeing him as if she'd thought they had some kind of *thing* going.

He got up and closed the door, returning to the chair, the leather squeaking as he sat. "You knew she was there and never said a word, didn't you, sir?"

"Of course. Just like I can see you sitting there naked."

"Oh, for fuck's sake!" Bishop looked around for something to cover himself with. Failing, he scooted the chair under the desk so at least his cock was hidden. "So what's next?"

"You know what's next, although there is a little job I need you to do before that. You find Waterman, deal with him and his men."

"Any news on that front?" Bishop picked up a pen and tapped it on the desk.

"They found your other hideout. Went inside, discovered nothing, because, of course, you'd gone. Our men arrived after they'd left, and *they* discovered a little gift inside. A warning to you, perhaps, or maybe it was just convenient for them to leave their package there."

"Package?"

"A man you knew as Kemp."

Bishop frowned. "So Kemp was waiting for me to return with Miss Jones?"

"No, Kemp was rather dead."

"What?"

Huntington chuckled. "He must have pissed Waterman off, who knows? Whatever, we disposed of him. Waterman owes us for cleaning up his mess. So when you catch up with him, give him a little more of what you're so good at, just so he *really* knows, before he meets his maker, that he annoyed us."

"You want Waterman *taken out?*" Christ, this was getting worse by the minute. He thought he'd have been asked to torture, to teach him a lesson, his usual thing. It was clear that whatever was inside those little bags Waterman had had delivered posed a massive risk to certain people — bigger than he'd first suspected.

"Yes, and Frankie Lash. This time you need to get your hands a little dirtier, I'm afraid. Waterman thinks he has every bag except the one you took, but he'll soon have a shock to find we've taken all of them from his men except one. You might want to go and fetch it. One of our other agents has been unable to collect."

"So? If he's unable to collect, what makes you think I'll do a better job of finding it?"

"Oh, we know where it is. The agent had a slight accident while trying to break in last night. Fell from a second-storey window. Broke his leg. Unfortunate, that."

"Right. Where is it?"

"In an apartment. East End. Unpleasant area, but there you go. Good hideout, nonetheless. Waterman has his head screwed on, stashing things in places the average person wouldn't think to check. But we're not average, are we?" He cleared his throat. "Glad to see you used the van and not the car to transport Miss Jones. You were found that way, you know. Like I said before, Waterman threatened a CCTV operator to give up your last whereabouts while in the car."

"How is the CCTV man?"

"You don't need to know."

"Right."

"So get to it. I'll send you the address in the usual manner. Oh, and leave the basement cameras on. I'll need to keep an eye on Miss Jones while you're gone."

Fucking pervert. "Okay, sir. Do you want me to bring the goods back here?"

"Yes. And we found the bag you picked up from the hotel. In the safe of your other place. Good job we did. Seems you forgot to take it with you when you left. Too busy wanting to keep Miss Jones safe, I fear."

Bishop cut the call without bothering to say anything more. He stood, conscious of being watched, and left the office. He glanced at Fallan, who pouted at him, curled up in one corner of the sofa, arms crossed over her breasts. Ignoring her, he strode into the bedroom, pulled some black clothes out of the wardrobe and dressed. He returned to the living room and picked up his discarded jeans, rummaging in the pocket for his mobile phone and the keys to this place and his van.

"Are we going somewhere?" she asked, tilting her head to one side and smiling.

"I am. You're staying here."

"What?" She sat upright, placing her hands on her knees, her smile vanishing. A rosy blush sprang to her cheeks.

Anger, he suspected.

He averted his attention to her breasts, cursing how she distracted him like that, then raised his gaze back to her face. "I have something I must do. You can't come with me—too dangerous." He jerked his head in the direction of the wall-mounted screens. "You'll be watched. You're safe. If you try to leave, you'll find that when you press for the lift you'll get an electric shock. It's pretty aggressive, will knock you back a few feet, probably land you on your arse."

She smirked, clearly disbelieving him. "So how come *you* didn't get a shock?"

"Because my boss saw us arrive and switched the device off, and when I leave it will go back on. Only someone who finds where to turn it off here would be able to operate the lift."

"I see. So I'm trapped here against my will."

"Something like that, although it doesn't appear to be against your will. Seems you enjoy spending time with me." Bishop shrugged on his jacket.

"I do, but, obviously, although *you* appear to enjoy spending time with *me*, I'm just a job, nothing more."

"That's right, Miss Jones." He had to say that, couldn't tell her anything else, couldn't afford to have her worm her way into his emotions any more than she could afford to have him in her life once he took her back where she belonged. Being the partner of a freelance government agent wasn't ideal for anyone. He didn't think she'd be able to handle it.

"Good," she said, surprising him. "At least we know where we stand. I'll fuck you while we're together — providing you want that, and anyway, it relieves the boredom, don't you know? — and then, when this shit's over, I'll continue with my life and you can get on with yours."

"That's right."

"But I'm thinking you owe me some money. I mean, if I'm going to lose that ten grand, you ought to pay me instead. I didn't ask to be here. I didn't know what I was getting into. I need that money."

"Fine."

She lifted her eyebrows. "Really?"

"Yes, really. Money in exchange for fucks. Classy." *Why did I say that?*

Hurt, in the form of a frown, crowded her forehead. "You fucking bastard. You really are a fucking bastard."

"I know, which is why, when you return to your regularly scheduled life, you'll want to forget all about me." *But I'll never forget you.* "So I have to go out. Not something that's ideally done in daylight, but needs must. Hopefully, by this time tomorrow you can go home. Oh, and you might want to find something to wear. Unless you like the thought of someone watching you while you're naked."

* * * *

Bishop sat in the van outside the target address. He pulled out his phone and checked the coded text message again, making sure he had the right place. Unfortunately he did. Getting inside through a window without being seen would be a nightmare. He'd have to go into the block of flats and gain entry that way. The building was...well, it was disgusting, gave council tenants a bad name. All right, most of those living in these kinds of areas were rough—the council housed them all together, made policing easier, the majority of crimes committed in the same place—but a few good, law-abiding folks also resided here and were tarnished by the dirty 'council rubbish' brush.

He sighed, knowing what he had to do and not wanting to do it. He slid his phone back into his pocket, then climbed over the front seat and into the back of the van. Taking the lid off a big plastic container, he grabbed a folded royal blue boiler suit and slipped it on over his clothes. Next, he took out a large makeup bag and crawled back into the driver's seat. Thankful for the tinted windows, he reached up to adjust the rear-view mirror so it reflected the lower half of his face. He opened the makeup bag and selected a fake bushy black beard and glue, then went about attaching it. As the glue dried, it pulled his skin taut, and he grimaced.

Fucking hate this part of the job.

He tilted the mirror down a little more and slapped on new eyebrows. Once the glue had dried, he popped in blue contact lenses, then slid on some ugly, clear-lens tortoiseshell glasses—the rectangular frames altering his appearance more than the facial hair. He reached into the glove compartment for a black beanie hat and jammed it on, tucking his hair inside. He lifted a rusty red toolbox from the passenger footwell. A gun and tools for breaking in were inside. As ready as he was ever going to be, he got out of the van, locked it, and walked towards the block of flats.

In the main foyer, a stark, grey-walled square that reeked of dried piss and vomit, he took the stairs, not wanting to chance getting stuck in the lift. The toolbox bounced against his leg with every step, and he muttered curses. On the second floor, he stared at the four front doors and took a deep breath to steady himself. Adrenaline had unleashed itself on his bloodstream and he needed a second or two to adjust. Confident, he inhaled deeply again then rapped on the third door, rehearsing his bullshit speech about being sent from the council to check the taps. He waited a moment, but with no response he lifted his hand to knock again.

On his left, the second door opened and a young woman with a baby perched on her hip appeared. Boy or girl child he didn't know — it only wore a nappy.

"He's not in," the woman said. "He was here last night, late, and before that, well, he isn't here often, put it that way. Seems like he only uses the place to stash stuff or have meetings every now and then with...women. And he's a right hard wanker. Wouldn't mess with him if I didn't have to."

"Oh, right." Bishop smiled. "Well, I've got to get in there. Leak's been reported." He placed the toolbox in front of the door so the back of it faced her, then hunkered down and opened it. He took out a lock-picking tool, closed the lid and stood.

"You allowed to do that?" she asked, eyeing the tool and repositioning the baby, who pulled on the woman's lank black hair. "I'm sure you're not allowed to go in. Says in my tenancy agreement that—"

"Yes, we have to give notice when we visit, but, in this case, when the flat downstairs might get flooded—"

"Fuck! Does Martha know? She's got kids in there. Last thing she'll need is water coming through the ceiling!"

"Which is why I have to go inside."

She nodded. "Right. Yeah, right. Well, I'll leave you to it."

She disappeared into her flat, and Bishop breathed easier, raising the tool to the keyhole and sliding it in. The fug of disuse slapped him in the face as he swung the door open, picked up his toolbox and stepped inside. He breathed through his mouth to prevent himself smelling the unpleasant, mixed odours of what appeared to be boiled cabbage and unflushed toilets. He pitied the women brought back here.

Slipping the lock-picking tool into a pocket in his boiler suit, he closed the door.

The flat was a state if the hallway was anything to go by. Whoever paid rent on this place didn't enjoy cleaning. He picked his way between coats slung on the floor and went through a doorway ahead, ignoring the one to his right. He stood in a kitchen where a dishwasher or use of hot soapy water in the sink was unheard of, wincing at plates covered in dried-on food scum and glasses bearing the remnants of milk and beer froth. He shuddered and shoved some crockery aside to place his toolbox on the work surface, remembering too late he hadn't put on any gloves. Once he'd covered his hands, he took a cloth from his box and went to the front door, wiping where he'd touched inside and out then closing himself in again and going back into the kitchen.

He made straight for the freezer, shifting packets and boxes around, looking for the tell-tale open food containers where a package could be stored. There weren't any, so he did the same with the fridge, recoiling at the stench of rancid milk. Nothing in there, either. He searched the cupboards and drawers, coming up empty-handed, so took his toolbox into the other room—a lounge—and began poking about in there.

Nothing.

Upstairs, he explored the smaller bedroom before going into the bathroom to check in a medicine cabinet, behind the bath panel, inside the electric shower casing, then under the lid of the toilet tank. He sighed in frustration, the beard itching like crazy and sweat dripping from his forehead into those infernal eyebrows. The little black pouch wasn't there.

Maybe that's what I'm doing wrong. Maybe it isn't in a pouch anymore. Fucking hell!

He stormed into the double bedroom, a corner of the toolbox once again bashing his leg, and he gritted his teeth to stave off the aching tenderness in his calf. He was shocked out of the pain upon seeing the bedroom tidy, a vast difference from the rest of the place. Perhaps the tenant did care about making the room presentable for the women he brought back here.

Who knows? Who fucking cares? I need that pouch and I'm gone.

The sound of the front door opening then closing had him tiptoeing to a built-in wardrobe spanning the entire wall opposite. He opened one of the louvered doors, praying the hinges didn't squeak, then shifted a small heap of dirty clothing across so he could stand inside. In the wardrobe, he put his toolbox on the washing then took out his gun, pleased he'd thought to attach a silencer. He closed the door. And waited, head hot beneath his hat.

Footsteps pounded the stairs. Despite having done this kind of job several times before, Bishop swallowed as his stomach rolled. The footsteps clunked on the landing. The sound of someone taking a piss filtered into the bedroom. Whoever had taken a leak didn't flush the toilet or turn on the tap so they could wash their hands. The person strode into the bedroom, a grey hooded jacket obscuring their features, went straight for the bedside cabinet nearest the door, and picked up the book on top.

Bishop peered harder through one of the slats, his nose nearly touching the wood. He steadied his breathing, conscious that it might breeze out with sound and alert the man he was there — and it *was* a man by the look of his size. The tenant stood side-on to Bishop, opened the book and pulled out a black velvet pouch, hidden in the cut-out pages.

Fuck, one of the oldest tricks and I didn't think…

Seemed there was a lot he didn't think about since he'd met Fallan.

The man looked inside the pouch and nodded, then slipped it into his hoodie pocket. He made for the wardrobe, and Bishop had a split second to take in who the man was and what he had to do. He readied his gun hand. Pushed open the louvered door. Took aim.

And shot Frankie fucking Lash in the centre of his forehead.

* * * *

Parked on a grass verge, Bishop sat in the van halfway to the second hideout, taking five minutes to himself. He'd tortured. He'd maimed. But he'd never fucking killed anyone before. He hadn't had much choice, though. Frankie's and Waterman's lives or his — that was the deal, that was his job. If he ran, the government would find him, of that he had no doubt. He'd been forced into being an assassin…and he knew in his gut that, after he'd killed Waterman, he'd have to kill more people. Once they knew he had, that he *would*, they'd ask him to do it again and again.

He took a deep breath, his mouth dry, and swallowed, grimacing at the aridity in his throat. He was fucked, good and proper, and his life as he'd known it was no more. He only hoped he didn't have nightmares, that guilt didn't take hold and cause him to make mistakes. He needed to think about what he'd done, accept it, then move on.

There wasn't any other option.

He thought of Fallan, waiting for him in the hideout, possibly worrying that he'd abandoned her, lied in saying he'd be coming back. He felt the need to go and see her, to take her somewhere else, but it was best they holed up there until he'd offed Waterman.

He didn't relish that one bit. Once done, it meant setting Fallan free.

Restarting the engine, he drove to the cottage and let himself in. Images of Frankie's eyes going wide and him falling back onto the bed, his brains splattering the quilt, would stay with Bishop forever, as would Bishop taking the pouch from Frankie's pocket and sliding it into his own. Fuck, Frankie had been a bastard, had killed people without a second thought, but he'd never done anything to Bishop. They'd got along when Bishop had been undercover, a part of Waterman's outfit.

Fuck, fuck, fuck. Stop tormenting yourself. It's done. Better it was him and not me.

But was it? What did he have to look forward to now? What woman in their right mind would want to settle down with a killer? What woman would want to spend time with him, accepting that he did a job he couldn't tell her much about, letting him go out there to earn a crust and not really knowing exactly what he was doing?

Fallan knows. It doesn't seem to bother her…

Don't even go there, pal. Do not even fucking go there.

Chapter Nine

Fallan had watched Bishop leave the basement apartment with bitter feelings. She understood this wasn't one of the usual occasions between a man and a woman, but, hey, a girl would like to hear some words of appreciation. No, it wasn't a hardship fucking him. The least he could do was pretend to feel something about what they'd shared together, though.

She'd mooched around, opening drawers and peering in cupboards. There were men's clothes in the wardrobe, all different sizes, as though several people used this place. She'd walked over to the lift door at one point, tempted to reach out and touch to see if he'd been telling the truth. Shaking her head from her stupidity, she'd stormed to the kitchen.

Now, with a coffee canister found, she began making herself a really strong brew. Even though she was 'only a job' she'd still continue to sleep with him. She liked spending time with him. For some strange reason she was comforted by his presence and enjoyed the way he made her feel. The sex was fantastic — there was no other word for it.

Once her drink was made, she turned round to view the rest of the room.

She dropped her coffee onto the floor as she stared at a man walking out of the lift. He wore a black suit, had salt-and-pepper hair, and stared at her with unnaturally piercing, bright blue eyes through nasty-arsed spectacles. He was overweight, his paunch telling her he ate well and possibly drank a lot of beer. Whoever it was must have been allowed in, given what Bishop had told her about the electric current having to be switched off…unless he'd been lying so she didn't try to escape.

"Who the fuck are you?" she said, stepping back from the mess on the floor.

"So your everyday language is just as bad as when you're in the throes of fucking," the man said, swiping a hand along the back of the chair where Bishop had been sitting earlier.

Had this man seen the action?

"If you're wanting to sell it as a porno, I want some of the cash," she told him, irate that the man clearly knew who she was, but she had no clue to his identity.

"It would certainly sell by the thousands. Pornos these days are all about the cum-shot. The women look half bored and are dry as bloody nuns. Maybe you and Bishop can charge your way into the industry. Call it 'Kidnapper Gets Fucked'?"

She had no idea who this fucker was but already knew she didn't like him. He should have *I'm a prick* written across his forehead.

"So pleased it was worth the watch." Cursing the mess on the floor, she bent down and began to pick up the shards.

"Are you stupid enough to turn your back on a man you know nothing about?" he asked, moving closer.

"For fuck's sake, what is it with you men? I wouldn't know the first thing to do to protect myself. Besides, Bishop said anyone coming through that door would be a good guy. At least I think he did. *Shit!*" she yelped. A piece of porcelain had cut into the base of her palm. "Fucking cock balls."

"You really do have a naughty mouth." He came over and took hold of her hand. "A small cut and there doesn't appear to be any china in there."

"Thank you for the diagnosis." She snatched her hand away.

"You really trust Bishop?"

"I've got no choice. He's taken me and now I can't leave until he decides I'm not some secret agent spy person." Walking to the kitchen area, she washed her hand under the cold tap, pressing a towel to the small cut. The bleeding stopped after a few seconds.

"Bright girl."

"No. I'm stupid. I shouldn't have thought for a second a ten-grand holiday was real. I'm in this mess because of greed...or need. Nothing more, nothing less." Fallan started the kettle back up. She grabbed a cloth and wiped up the last of the spillage from the floor. "Are you staying for coffee?"

"You don't even know my name yet."

She didn't want to know it. "And don't expect a fuck, either. I figure you'll tell me your name when you're comfortable doing so. Well, do you want one?"

"What? A fuck or a coffee?"

"A coffee, arsehole."

"Yes."

In no time at all she had made him a drink. Then she went and sat on the chair in the living area. She wouldn't have felt comfortable with him sitting there. She'd been intimate on it with another man only an hour or so ago.

He sat on the sofa. Not caring about his attention on her, she turned the television on and tried to blank him out. If he wasn't going to talk, she wouldn't try to initiate conversation. Some show about DNA testing came on. The drama would be more welcome than the tense silence.

Despite trying to switch her mind off her situation, Fallan thought about the man. Could he be a vicious killer? He looked harmless…but, then, so did Bishop.

"Are you really into television shows?" he asked.

"Not usually. I'm normally at work listening to the beep-beep-beep of a supermarket till."

"What did you do?" he asked.

"I'm sure Bishop has told you everything about me." She turned the volume up, hoping he'd get the message and be quiet.

About half an hour had gone by before he spoke again. "My name's Huntington."

"Nice to meet you," she said as a greeting.

"I can see why he likes you."

"Who?"

"You know who," he answered.

"Bishop? No, I imagine he likes the regular sex but he doesn't like me."

"From the clips last night I'd say he's got a thing for you." Huntington eased back into his seat, staring across at her.

"Okay, you want to talk?" Fallan turned the sound to mute and placed the remote on the arm of the chair.

"Not particularly."

"I can see you're itching to interrogate me. We've got coffee and time, might as well use the opportunity." She picked up her cup and waited, shocked by the fact she wasn't afraid.

"What was in the bag?" Tough guy, went straight for the kill.

"I don't know. As I told your man, I accepted a holiday as I was strapped for cash. A treasure hunt game, several other women were in on it."

He kept firing the questions at her. Sometimes the same questions but in a different way. Almost like he was trying to trick her into admitting something.

An hour went by and she made more coffee, enjoying his company even if the conversation was all to find out more about her past.

"Have I passed the test yet?" she asked after she'd replied to his latest question. Since when was having a happy childhood important?

"Fuck me. Bishop sure knows where to find them. You must be the single most innocent woman I've met. And you've got a great arse." Huntington rose from the sofa and stood behind her chair.

So intent on how to answer his question, she hadn't heard the lift door go. Bishop stood in the lift doorway, wearing a blue boiler suit, a fuck-off bushy beard and eyebrows, and a pair of spectacles similar to Huntington's. What the hell? Did he think he wouldn't be recognised like that? She'd know him anywhere. Fallan wanted to run into his arms and hug him. He looked pale and drawn as if years had been added on to his age.

"Are you all right?" she asked.

Bishop nodded but didn't look at her. His gaze was firmly planted on Huntington.

Seeing the undercurrent of tension, she excused herself and went through to the bedroom to give the men their privacy.

* * * *

Fallan didn't know how long the men had been sitting in the other room, but she'd changed into a dressing gown in the meantime. Bishop came into the bedroom a while later looking worse than when he'd entered the basement.

"Are you all right?" she asked again, wondering where he'd been with that facial hair.

He hesitated, taking off the spectacles and putting them on a chest of drawers. He fiddled with his eyes, popping out contacts and placing them beside the specs. Moving from her position on the bed, she stood in front of him. Bishop didn't appear to be the confident man she'd grown accustomed to.

"I don't want to talk about it." He stalked to the shower.

Frowning, Fallan let him go. Something was up. He didn't even have any of his usual distrustful questions to throw at her.

"I can't do this," she said to herself.

He clearly had something on his mind and needed time alone. How could she help him deal with whatever was plaguing him?

Why would she even *want* to help him?

The wires inside her head were starting to cross. He'd kidnapped her, forced her from one house to another, and now here she stood, caring about a man who only viewed her as a fucking job.

Even knowing all this, you still want to please him, don't you, Fallan?

She would very much like to growl at her own mind.

Weighing up the points pissed her off. Why couldn't she just accept her situation and think of Bishop as a very grumpy boyfriend who had a large cock and knew how to use it?

That sorted, she sat on the bed and thought of the best way to ease Bishop's mind from his troubled thoughts.

She glanced into a mirror on the wall for a hair and body check. Thoughts of their sexual time together brought enough moisture to her folds she wouldn't have to worry about faking it. With Bishop she never wanted to fake an orgasm. She wanted to enjoy her time with him. She'd get herself ready so she was waiting for him when he came back into the bedroom.

Twenty minutes later, he came out of the shower, sans beard and eyebrows, with a towel wrapped around his middle and another he was using to dry his hair. Fallan had decided on a kneeling position beside the bed. She bowed her head, face almost touching the floor. She'd heard some stuff about submission and figured with his high-end, double-secret shitty job he wouldn't want a tiring woman in his life. Opening her mind, she imagined her husband had come home from work and she was there to do his bidding.

"What the fuck is this?" he asked.

Turning her nose up at a small tumbleweed of dust on the floor and going cross-eyed trying to keep with her performance of a submissive, she paced herself for a few seconds then responded to him.

"I'm a gift from your trying day," she croaked out, wincing at how bad and corny her words sounded. She should have spent the time while he was in the shower rehearsing lines.

"I've not got time for games," he growled.

"Permission to stand, Sir?" she asked, staying in character.

"Fallan, this is—"

"Permission to stand, Sir?" *I don't give a fuck if you don't want to play. I do, and you'll fucking play. Don't say that out loud, Fallan. Remember this is for him.*

"Stand."

Okay, so she was going to have to work to get him in the mood. Not a hardship, but, still, it would have been nicer if he'd wanted to play.

Maybe she could get him to say a few naughty words to her?

"You're so wet. I'm going to get you nice and dry," she said, still with her gaze fixed on the floor. Careful to not walk into anything, she took the towel from his hand and began to dry his body. "You're such a brave man going out into the world like that." Where were these lines coming from?

"I'm a brave man."

What was that? Is he participating?

"Would my Master like a nice view while I finish drying his body?"

"He would like that very much."

Yes! I got him.

Untying the sash of her dressing gown, she eased it open and let it fall to the floor for dramatic effect. Her body was on fire from talking the words out.

He hissed and she smiled.

She returned to drying his upper body, arms, chest, neck and hair before she dropped the towel. Glancing down at the one around his hips, she contained a giggle when she saw it tented at his groin. Bishop wasn't immune to a little role-playing, then.

"Do I own you?" he asked.

"For now I'm your slave to do with as you wish."

He touched her face, tilting her head back, and ran his thumb over her mouth. Leaning in, Fallan puckered her lips but no kiss came.

"I don't want to kiss you. Not this time," he said.

Disappointed, she masked her emotion quickly, not wanting him to be annoyed with her.

"In fact, all I want to do is fuck this lovely body."

He tore the towel from his hips and walked her back to the edge of the bed. She fell with a laugh then moaned as he tugged a tight nipple into his mouth.

"Harder," she gasped.

"I'm the Master. You'll do as *I* say." He bit down on her nipple a little harder, seeking her moist slit with his hand.

Fallan cried out from the pain in her nipple to the pleasure from his fingers. She was so close to orgasming.

"Don't come yet," he warned.

She cried out again, hating her own game. Why was it men always wanted the women to hold off from climaxing? Was it jealousy, seeing as they could only climax once throughout a session?

Whatever it was, she was pissed off because of it. Instead of voicing her protest, though, she lay prone beneath him, enjoying his hands and mouth even if she couldn't enjoy the ultimate benefit of what he could do with them.

He lifted his head and glanced at her. She saw the battle warring within him.

"What's the matter?" she asked.

"I want to fuck you."

"I've not got a problem with that," she told him, smiling.

"No, I want to fuck you hard."

"I'm not going anywhere. Do what you want." To help convince him she meant what she'd said, she opened her legs wide for him to see all of her exposed cunt flesh.

Bishop continued to stare at her. She sucked on her finger then placed it against her clit.

"I want it," she said on a moan.

He grasped his cock and pressed the tip to her entrance. For however long it took before she was allowed to come, all Fallan could do was hold on.

He didn't push inside but pulled her to the edge of the bed and held her hips at an upward angle. Kneeling on the floor, he gripped her hips tighter and thrust all the way inside her. Before she could catch her breath, he withdrew then slammed back in. Nothing soft or nice, but dirty and hard.

She screamed with a force that shocked her. He pounded into her. There was no pain, only the most exquisite torture of pleasure Fallan had ever experienced. She didn't want it to end. She grabbed the sheets, holding them in her fists. His pelvis rubbed against her clit — a wonderful sensation.

"Can I come?" she begged, wanting…no, *needing* the release of orgasm.

"Yes," he snapped, each thrust designed to send her further over the edge than the last.

He tilted back and up, hitting a spot inside her, forcing her lower half further up. Reaching out, she pulled him down for a kiss. No longer would she be denied the pleasure of his lips. He pummelled deep inside her over and over that spot, making her mindless. She wedged one hand between them and pressed a finger to her clit, taking her over the edge to sweet oblivion. Her pussy tightened and she panted through the bliss. He jerked harder than before. With one long, hard plunge he erupted inside her, a loud growl spilling from his lips.

Bishop stayed in that position for some time until he pulled out of her and collapsed on the bed, covering his eyes with one hand. Not bothering to cover herself, she crawled up beside him.

She didn't say anything and lay waiting.

"Thank you," he whispered.

"Anytime."

He rolled over and faced her. "I didn't hurt you, did I?"

She was touched with how concerned he was but he didn't need to be. "I'm fine. More than fine."

"I lost control." He placed a hand on her stomach and made to move as if he was going to look down and examine her.

She stopped him. "I said I'm fine. I wouldn't have come if I didn't enjoy it."

"I don't know what I'd do if I hurt you."

Was he aware of what his words meant to her? Did he feel something more for her than the fucking?

"You'll never hurt me. I know that." She brought him in against her body and kissed his temple. She rested his head on her breast and stroked his hair.

Staring at the ceiling, she waited again, her body covered in a fine sheen of sweat. She wanted to get up and shower.

He shifted his fingers, lightly caressing her belly. She let him.

"I killed a man today," he said after a long stretch of silence.

"I know." Fallan didn't know how she did but she'd sensed a change in him. One that didn't sit well with him.

"I've never killed anyone before."

That confession surprised her.

"I don't know if you'll consider me any worse for it, but I usually only torture people for information. I guess a clean death is more suited than where you pray for death before it's granted."

Fallan stroked his hair some more. A tear fell from her eye. "Is that why Huntington was here? To make sure you'd finished the job?"

"I doubt it. No one ever knows what's going on in Huntington's mind until he wants to tell you. He didn't try anything, did he?"

"Besides ask a billion questions? He was the perfect gentleman."

Silence descended on them again for a few minutes. Fallan tried to process what he'd told her. He'd never taken another person's life before today but he had tortured them.

"That stuff in the bag? You know, the one I was fooled into planting?"

He nodded.

"Was it really bad? I mean, was there information in it that would hurt someone? It wasn't protecting anyone who'd done bad things?"

"I can't tell you everything."

"I know, but please tell me I wasn't involved with anything to do with drugs or prostitution, or—oh God, this makes me sick to my stomach—child pornography?"

"No. Don't worry, it has nothing to do with any of that."

"But if I knew what it was it could get me killed?"

"Go to sleep, Fallan."

She had her answer.

Chapter Ten

Dusk had been making an appearance as Huntington had left the cottage. Back in his office now, he withdrew the recording device from his inside jacket pocket and placed it on the desk. He wasn't sure he could listen to it without having a stiff brandy first. Bishop had pissed him off, no doubt about it, but Huntington had laid the cards very firmly on the table — Bishop had to continue doing his job, with the addition of killing where necessary, or lose his life.

Simple.

Huntington took off his suit jacket and hung it over the straight-backed chair in the corner, the one he used for interviewing — he preferred that term to interrogating — those who needed a little persuasion to do what he expected of them. He grimaced at the thought of Bishop sitting in it. That man would know why Huntington had chosen the chair and the result wouldn't be Bishop cowering and obeying every request — not without a few questions and making it clear he wasn't happy, anyway. He had got too big for his bloody boots. Needed taking down a peg or two. But he was a damn good agent—their best—and losing him would be a big blow.

Pouring a brandy from a crystal decanter he'd been given for twenty years of secret government service, he took a sip and relished the burn as the liquid went down his throat. It hit his belly and warmed there, heat spreading to his limbs, relaxing them and his mind. He locked the door, then sat at his desk and toed off his shoes, confident the next phase would happen. Bishop would go for Waterman and whoever else got in the way, he was sure. This mission would be over soon. They had all the bags—he'd taken the final one from Bishop earlier. The government people involved were safe...and the information in those bags wouldn't hurt to be used as a little leverage if those people chose to play up in the future. The only blot on the landscape now was Waterman and his crew, or what was left of it.

And maybe Bishop. I'll have to keep an eye on him.

He sipped again, leaning back in his chair and closing his eyes. Bishop really was becoming a problem. Before, he'd done as he was asked, threatened a few people, secured whatever needed collecting or reclaiming, and did whatever the hell he did in his spare time. But now? Huntington grimaced. That woman had changed him, made him want what he couldn't have—a normal life.

She was beautiful, he'd give him that. Could see why Bishop had fallen for her. And he had, despite his denials. Huntington gathered Bishop had lied to him about his feelings in order to keep her safe, so when she was returned to her regular life she'd be left to melt into society again, an inconsequential woman who didn't need watching.

I don't think she does, either. She just wants her money, wants to go home and fix her life.

But what if spending more time with Bishop changed that?

He flicked on a monitor to his left and expected nothing more than the blank screen he got. Bishop had switched off the basement cameras, and Huntington wondered whether they were fucking now or had finished. Or perhaps they hadn't even started. He'd told Bishop to get some rest before tonight. Waterman was best taken out under cover of darkness.

He picked up his secure phone and dialled. "Anything?"

"No," said the agent. "Just the residents coming and going."

"So Bishop did his job, then," he said more to himself than to the agent. "Good. No visitors?"

"Not for the deceased, as far as I can tell. Just the usual rough lot who live around here."

"Right. Call in if anything changes."

"Will do."

Replacing the receiver in the cradle, Huntington swigged another gulp of brandy and wondered when Waterman would discover Lash wasn't going to be reporting in for work any time soon. The agent stationed outside Lash's flat had to wait until about four a.m.—that crucial time where drug pushers finally went to sleep and burglars hadn't yet woken for their early morning raids—before he could make a move and dispose of the body. One hour, plenty of time.

Sighing, he reached for the recording device and turned it on.

"Frankie Lash is dead, if that's what you're here to find out," Bishop said.

"Good, but no, that wasn't the purpose of my visit."

"What was, then? Planting a new bug I'm meant to be unaware of? Reckon I'll tell Fallan everything, give her information she can go to the papers with? The *government* with?" Bishop's laugh sounded more sinister the second time around.

"No, I came to see Miss Jones for myself. It's all very well having a report from you that she's a good woman, but appearances can be so very deceptive, can't they." Huntington had meant it as a statement, a bold fact that he'd wanted Bishop to take the way he had.

"If you're referring to me in an underhand way, Huntington, just come out and say what you have to say. I'm not into fucking about, dancing around the issue, you know that. I'm a big boy. I can take it."

"All right. I think you're going to go off the rails. I think Miss Jones has affected you, affected how you think, and your future performances may be in jeopardy because of it."

Bishop huffed. "I told you, she's just a fucking job, nothing more."

"A fucking job—exactly. That's the problem. You've fucked her, got *involved* with a person who is a part of this mission. That isn't allowed, you *know* that. Fuck whoever the hell else you want, but your sexual partners must remain oblivious to what we do—to what *you* do. You've allowed emotions—"

"The only emotions involved with her are those I get when I'm coming, all right? That blunt enough for you?"

"It'll do for now."

A shuffle sounded where Huntington had risen from the sofa to pace the room. "So explain this. She's seen you in disguise, knew exactly who you were when you walked in. How *is* that? Did you tell her somehow what you'd be changing into for the Lash job?"

"No, I fucking didn't! Watch the tapes, listen to them. At no point did I tell her that."

"So how did she know it was you, before you even spoke?"

"I don't fucking know, do I? Jesus. Maybe she recognised the way I walk, my hands, the shape of my eyes, I don't know. Whatever—she won't be seeing me again once she goes home, will she? Doesn't know my real name, doesn't even know where the first hideout is, or this one. Your name's as much of a fake as mine. So, she's none the wiser. She'll go home, pay her bills—because I'll be giving her the ten grand myself if you don't—and eventually forget all about this."

"I doubt it. Who could forget being kidnapped and fucked by her abductor?"

"Are you implying something? It wasn't forced, nothing like that."

"I know. I heard. Saw."

"So you did."

Huntington reflected now on how Bishop had said that. Three words etched with lashings of disgust.

He really does care for her. Fuck it!

Another shuffle where Huntington had walked over to the kitchen area and poured himself a glass of water, his tongue furry from too much of Miss Jones' coffee. "You need information about tonight, Bishop. Listen to me very carefully. Miss Jones must *not* know what you're doing. She mustn't know what you've already done, understand?"

Bishop sighed. "Yep. Go on."

"First, get some sleep. It might be a long night. I'll call you with any information I get after I return to the office, but, if there is none, you'll need to stake out Waterman's place of business. We know he's never home in the evenings, but we'll post another agent there nevertheless. Once you deem it's safe enough, go inside. Usual drill at first—find out whatever you can. Then do whatever you have to do. Once your job is complete, come back here and report to me."

"Exactly as I thought it would be. I'm not happy about this new turn of events, I have to tell you that."

"I know you're not, but, like I told you before, it's them or you, right?" Huntington had paused, a thought striking him, and he went back to the sofa. He'd leant forward, studying Bishop for signs of dissent. "Tell me, what would you have felt like before meeting Miss Jones?"

"What do you mean?"

"Your job description changing. Would you have refused to take anyone out? The way I see it, you had no one, nothing to live for, so us making you…disappear wouldn't have been so bad. But now? Well, you have a little woman in there"—Huntington had tapped his temple then his chest, over his heart—"and us removing you from any and every equation suddenly isn't an option, is it?"

"Oh, fuck right off. Don't try and make this out to be something it isn't. I may not have had much of a life before she came along, but I had one and I don't fancy dying. I'd have killed for you, all right? She has nothing to do with this, and I'm getting hacked off with telling you that."

"All right!" Huntington had raised his hands. "All right. I believe you."

He didn't.

Huntington switched off the recorder, mulling over the options. If Bishop continued seeing Miss Jones after mission completion, there would be no other choice but to have the woman taken out.

Unless…

Hmmm. I'll think on it. She may very well make a damn fine agent if she learns to keep that rowdy mouth of hers shut.

* * * *

Waterman frowned. Frankie wasn't answering his mobile phone — unusual for him, even when he was fucking a prozzer — and if he was doing some tart on work time, Waterman would have something to say about it.

He called his other employees — all out doing their usual jobs of collecting protection money, duffing a few people up, the normal things his crew tended to do, as well as keeping their ears to the ground as to that bastard Rook's whereabouts. It pissed him off he still didn't know the man's name — his real one, not the moniker he'd used when working for Waterman. He needed sorting, that one, erasing permanently. Frankie was meant to have gone to his hideout flat, picked up the goods and returned by now. Then he was supposed to have been out looking for Rook. Fucking Lash wanker was probably shagging some bitch.

I swear to God, if he is…

He tried Frankie's phone again. No answer. He hung up then redialled, just a jab on one button. "Can you come up to my office?" No please, no thank you…no need. His employees did as they were fucking told or they were gone.

Waterman waited. A knock came a couple of minutes later, and he straightened in his chair. "Come in."

What's-his-name opened the door and walked in, standing until Waterman nodded in the direction of the chair in front of his desk. What's-his-name closed the door then sat, looking as though he was about to crap his pants.

"I need you to do me a favour," Waterman said, eyeing the man, sizing him up.

"Yes, sir?"

"What's your name again?"

"Gavin Brent, sir."

"Gavin Brent, right. Gavin, all my men are busy. Kemp's no longer on my payroll, as you know, and Frankie seems to be unreachable. Looks like I'm going to have to go to Frankie's flat myself. Trouble is, it's a rough area, know what I mean? You comfortable taking me?" Waterman didn't care about the man's comfort, didn't care whether he wanted to go or not. He'd be going.

"All right," Gavin said. "Shall I wait outside for you then bring you back?"

"Uh, no. This isn't that kind of pick-up. I need you to actually go to his flat and knock on the door. I'll be coming with you. Call yourself my protection, if you like. You know, bodyguard."

Gavin puffed out his chest. Waterman reckoned the bloke would do nicely as one of his right-hand men, given a bit of training. He nodded absently. Yeah, he liked that idea.

"Yes, sir. Fine, sir."

"Good man." Waterman glanced at his watch. Fucking nine o'clock already. Where the hell was Frankie? He'd left to collect the bag hours ago.

Waterman shrugged. Maybe Lash had decided to have a nap, the cheeky fucker. "I'll give the tosser another hour to finish shagging his bitch or whatever the hell he's doing, then we'll go, okay?"

"Yes, sir."

"Off you go, then. Make yourself a cuppa. A bit of something to eat, yeah?"

"Yes, sir, thank you." Gavin rose and left the room.

Waterman waited for the door to click closed before he picked up his phone again. He dialled Frankie's number, anger starting a slow burn inside him. Yeah, he'd been mildly annoyed before, but now he was getting a bit narked—more than a bit narked. If Frankie didn't come waltzing in here within the hour, stupid grin on his ugly mug, then Waterman would have to accept that either something was dodgy or Frankie had run into a bit of trouble.

Chapter Eleven

The phone trilling jarred Bishop awake. He stared at the dark ceiling for a second or two, disoriented as to where he was. Then he remembered, and everything came crashing back. The red phone-alert light mounted above the door blinked along with every ring. He got out of bed, checking that Fallan remained asleep, then strode through the living area and into the office, comfortable about being naked because the cameras were still off.

"Hello?" he said upon answering, knowing it was Huntington.

"Get ready. Now. You need to have left ten minutes ago."

"I have plenty of time. It's only ten-fifteen. Waterman won't be alone until at least — "

"Things have changed. Waterman's just pulled up with his driver outside Lash's flat."

"Jesus."

"Yes, so you need to get there fast."

"How do you know this?"

"Does it matter?"

"Yes, it fucking does, because if you've got an agent posted outside that flat feeding you information, why can't the agent do the job?"

"Because I want you to do it."

Bastard.

"You're one sick fuck, Huntington."

"Don't you want to get him back for what you witnessed him doing when you were undercover there? All those young girls forced into the sex trade… Hmm?"

Bishop gritted his teeth.

"And," Huntington said, "you know what happens if you don't do what I ask. And who knows *what* might befall Miss Jones without you around…?"

Bishop held off calling his boss a wanker — the man would probably get pleasure from it. "I'm on it."

"Hurry up."

Bishop cut the call then returned to the bedroom, dressing quickly in his blue boiler suit. He didn't have time to attach the facial hair so slapped on the spectacles and the beanie hat, hoping they'd be sufficient in securing his true identity. He knelt beside the bed to place a soft kiss on Fallan's temple, then went to the kitchen and wrote a note.

Gone to work. Be back soon, B.

He almost laughed a little too loudly at the absurdity of that. What, did he think she'd give a shit where he'd gone, when he'd be back? All she wanted was to go home and pay off her debts, and he couldn't blame her. Yet something inside him said she would care, but he couldn't dwell on that now. He'd get this job done to keep her safe and for no other reason. Yes, Waterman was a bad seed, but he'd been under observation for a long time, and those young girls had been removed from where they'd been placed hours after being put there. They were safe. Huntington didn't need to give Bishop an excuse to help him ease any guilt he might feel when killing Waterman. Fallan's safety was plenty reason enough.

He left the note on the counter then, in the office, switched on the cameras. If it meant Huntington perved on her while she slept, so be it. In the lift, he went through what he'd have to do, flirting with different scenarios so he always had a back-up plan should things take a different turn from what he'd expected. Leaving the cottage in the van that someone might well recognise from his earlier visit, he steadied his nerves with a few deep breaths. It was dark now, and if the residents of the East End had any sense, they wouldn't bother looking out of their flat windows at night. Not with the deals going down on the street outside, being witnesses to goings-on they didn't need to see.

On the road, he mentally checked his toolbox. The gun was still loaded from last time, and, hopefully, if things went well, he wouldn't need to reload. Still, he'd make sure he had extra ammunition in his pocket, just in case.

He reached the housing estate Lash lived on seventeen minutes later and parked behind a battered, moss-green Ford Mondeo. It fitted the surroundings, and he guessed the driver was a government agent or a drug pusher. He reached for his toolbox, taking out his gun and extra bullets, sliding both into the inside pocket of an old black leather jacket on the passenger seat. After putting it on, he checked his face in the rear-view mirror then left the van. He walked along the path, glancing into the Mondeo, receiving a nod from the unkempt driver, noting the butt of a gun poking out of the glovebox. Satisfied his back was covered, Bishop headed for the flats, taking the same route as he had before. Once he reached the top of the stairs on the second floor, though, he paused to scope out the hallway.

All the doors were closed. He sidled along the wall opposite them until he stood in front of Lash's. He stepped forward and pressed his ear to the door. Muffled sounds came from inside, grunting from someone and faint orders from another — Waterman, if he wasn't mistaken. He turned the handle, relieved when the door opened, and peeped through the crack. Seeing no one, he went inside, closing the door quietly.

They were upstairs — the shuffling footsteps and talking told him that — and, if he remembered correctly, judging by where the noises were coming from, they were in Lash's bedroom. He briefly wondered what Waterman's expression had been like upon discovering Frankie with a bullet hole in his forehead, his brains plastered all over the bed. Not a happy man, he'd bet.

Taking a deep breath and getting out his gun, he moved to the foot of the stairs and looked up. Shadows played on the wall, a macabre dance of arms and fingers and the unmistakeable shape of someone holding a body beneath its armpits. They'd be on the landing any second, so he withdrew to the living room, hiding behind the door.

"Get him the fuck downstairs! I don't care whether you want to or not!" Waterman bellowed.

Clonking soon followed, Bishop guessing it was Frankie's feet smacking each step as Waterman's goon hauled the body down the stairs. He stared through the crack in the door, just below the top hinge, his breathing stuttered and his heartbeat going way too fast. Adrenaline surged through him, making him momentarily giddy, and he blinked to regain focus.

A man came into view, walking down backwards, his black suit crumpled behind the knees. Lash's body was somewhat stiff. Rigor mortis had started, then, which would make it difficult for Waterman and his employee to make Frankie's removal look casual, like he was drunk and they were just carrying him to the car. A stiffening body would put paid to that idea.

The man, one Bishop hadn't met when 'working' for Waterman, was dressed in a suit, a flat peaked cap on his head, slightly askew, the badge on the front denoting him as a driver. What the hell was going on if Waterman had to resort to using a man who wasn't used to this sort of shit? When he'd been in Waterman's employ, a driver was just that—unversed in violence and there to cart Waterman from one place to the next. Then he remembered Kemp was also dead and wondered if Waterman's mob wasn't as well ordered as he'd thought.

"Take him into the living room," Waterman instructed, coming down the stairs.

Bishop's heart rate accelerated further, and he thanked whatever entity was listening—things were going his way. With any luck, he'd have no trouble here and could leave the mess behind for someone else to clean up.

The man dragged Frankie into the living room, puffing and panting, a hitched sob tacked on to the end for good measure. Bishop pressed himself against the wall, easing the door closer to him and hoping the man was occupied enough that he wouldn't see it moving. Bishop glanced to the side, through the crack again, and shuddered at the sight of Waterman rounding the newel post and heading for the living room door. He hated him, no question, but he didn't relish killing the man. Yes, Waterman was a bastard, did a lot of damage to a lot of people, but... No, Bishop had to get rid of him. He had no choice. If he didn't, Waterman would kill *him*, leaving Fallan at the mercy of Huntington who, Bishop had no doubt, would use her for fucking...or worse.

He couldn't allow that to happen.

And as for the driver? Was he innocent, literally just a driver, working for a man he hadn't realised until now was a bad lot? Did he have a wife and kids waiting at home, relying on him to bring home the bacon?

He didn't want to think about that.

Waterman was in the room now. Bishop dared to peer around the edge of the door. Both men stood with their backs to him, staring down at the mess Frankie Lash had become. Bishop almost heaved at the sight — one he'd created.

Fuck.

Frankie's skin was a mottled grey. Purple splotches marred his cheeks and forehead. Blood matted his hair, the tufts sticking up in all directions, sprinkles of dried brain in places. His hands were stuck in stars, maybe from his shock at coming face to face with a gunman, remaining that way because he'd been shot so fast he didn't have time to change their position. His mouth was a skewed circle, the shape reminding Bishop of the globs of wax in those rocket-like lamps that had come back into fashion a few years ago.

"Rolling him up in a rug's out," Waterman said. "It'd look dodgy."

The driver rubbed his forehead with his fingertips. "I didn't sign up for this, sir."

"I know you didn't, but I did tell you when you started you might be needed for other things, and I distinctly remember you assuring me you'd help out anywhere you were needed. Ain't that right, Gavin Brent of 67 Fringley Road—where a wife and three little kiddies dwell, safe for the moment, safer still when you do what I fucking tell you? Are you getting me?"

"Yes, sir."

"So, break his arms and legs, then we can be on our way."

"What?" The driver looked up, showing Bishop his profile. His mouth shape matched Frankie's, and his eyes were wide and watery.

"You heard me," Waterman said, rolling his shoulders. "Break his fucking legs. We can't carry him out like that, can we? He'll be stiff as a damn board soon if we take any longer. People'll start to wonder, but if he's floppy...then we're talking."

Bishop couldn't handle watching. Yes, he'd broken legs in the past, but never on a dead body. That didn't make it any better, but—

He raised his gun, aimed at the back of Waterman's head and fired, the report nothing but a loud puff of air because of the silencer.

Waterman lurched forward, the inside of his head finding its way to the opposite wall, a red and black mural on a cream expanse. He went down, his top half landing on the sofa, legs sprawled over Frankie's torso. Somewhere in the distance was a male scream, and Bishop realised he'd entered some kind of zone where sound was dulled. It was the driver, who gaped at Waterman then slapped a hand over his mouth.

"Don't," Bishop said, automatically going into work mode. He came out from behind the door, true sound returning. "Don't puke. If the police arrive before my people, *because you screamed*, they might be able to identify you from your vomit, along with any hairs and skin cells you've left behind. Very silly of you not to wear gloves, don't you think?"

The driver twisted to face him, expression one of horror and confusion, hair soaked from what Bishop guessed was a sudden bout of sweating.

"I didn't... I wasn't... This isn't—" His eyes darted from side to side, gaze finally settling on the doorway.

Bishop read him easily. The man was getting ready to bolt.

"I know." Bishop trained the gun on him, level with his chest. "Nevertheless, if you want to remain safe, you'll have to come with me."

"But I...I'm just a driver. This wasn't... I didn't realise... I won't tell anyone, I swear. I—"

"Be quiet." Bishop jerked the gun in the direction of the door. "Now move. Nice and slowly. We're going to go downstairs, go outside. There's a car out there. You're going to get in it."

"But Mr Waterman's car. What about that?"

"That's the least of your worries. Now go. One wrong move and your head's mine, got it?"

The driver nodded while heading for the front door. He opened it, cuffing his nose with his free hand, which shook. He walked like a good citizen, down the stairs, into the piss-riddled foyer, and out into the night. They made it to the kerb without encountering anyone. At the Mondeo, Bishop opened the rear door and shoved the man inside. To the agent, he said through the open car window, "I did what I had to do, but I'm not sorting this bloke here. Find someone else. And Waterman's car will need returning to his offices."

He strode away and climbed in the van. Started the engine. Drove off.

Back to Fallan.

Chapter Twelve

Fallan moaned as she rolled over. Her body was sore in a deliciously sinful kind of way. For so long she'd woken up knowing she'd been all alone, all night long, but now she could smile. She had a man. Bishop wasn't your typical man, but he still had a dick and knew how to use that monster.

She pulled the blanket away from her body and saw the handprint bruises he'd made on her hips. The bruises, a true mark of his possession. What on earth was she thinking? How could she have begun to imagine Bishop as being her boyfriend? The man was a contracted agent for the government who'd abducted her. He'd said she was nothing more than a job to him—someone to play with to pass the time while on a mission, she guessed. She'd known that, should accept it, but he was so goddamned 'her type' she'd allowed herself to slip into the 'What if?' game.

Dangerous.

Just because she happened to like being with him didn't make the guy hers. Did it? Ugh, she needed some coffee. For first thing after waking this was some heavy shit to think about.

Would she want Bishop as a full-time, long-term boyfriend? What if he was the kind of guy who'd get everything wrong? Forget her birthday and Valentine's Day? What good would he be when going to the parents' for Sunday lunch...?

Hold on... She didn't need to worry about parents. Both of hers were dead. She didn't believe in Valentine's Day — she preferred love to be shown all year round not just on one day. And who wanted to celebrate the fact they were getting older?

"This is too much. I need coffee," she growled.

It wasn't a great surprise to find the bed empty. She imagined Bishop would never admit he liked a cuddle after sex. He would lie about it if she asked, saying he preferred a fuck just like her and that was that, but she sensed the truth. No way could a man hold her as tightly as he had and hate snuggles.

Naked, Fallan walked through to the kitchen. A coffee pot was already at work, plopping drips of brew through freshly ground beans into the glass carafe below. The scent was an aphrodisiac to her senses. As she went to grab some powdered creamer from a cupboard, she found a note from Bishop.

Gone to work. Be back soon, B.

A chuckle escaped from her lips. They were at the 'I'm leaving but not without letting you know' stage. A warm, fuzzy feeling engulfed her. She held the note and kept reading the words. She thought it was cute how he'd signed the letter — *B.* How he'd set the coffee on for when she awoke. He might give the impression he was a hard-hearted bastard, but what hard-hearted bastard prepared coffee for the woman he was currently fucking if he didn't give a shit about her?

Coffee cup in hand, she walked back to the bedroom and, feeling all domesticated, she cleaned their mess.

The bed made and the clothes taken care of, she found a washing machine and tumble drier in a small utility room off the kitchen, beside the office.

I could get used to this. Being with him. Caring for him…

Fallan shocked herself with how easy it had been, and, in such short time, to fall for a man and be at his beck and call. Already, even not having known Bishop long, she knew she'd do anything he asked. Part of her trusted him more than she had ever trusted anyone in her entire life.

That must be wrong. She normally depended on no one but herself to stay safe and make it through the muddles in her world, working and paying the bills.

Those sad, morose thoughts interrupted her cheery mood and she slammed the cup in the porcelain sink, smashing the cup.

"Shit."

She couldn't deal with this…this bullshit dream world. Any minute he'd come back with the intent of sending her on her way. Job done, off you go now, Miss Jones. Nice knowing you—fucking you—but we're done. Next! No thank you or long, sweet goodbye. Their time together would be completely over.

But she didn't want it to end. She could picture their life together in this basement—a small place to make love and work together for a future, hidden below a cottage where no one knew where they were and they could indulge in one another with no interruptions.

Bishop might be an enigma at the moment, but he *must* crave the same things she did. Didn't everyone want happiness with someone they loved? Before meeting him she'd never thought of settling down and having a family, but with him she could do it. How the fuck had that happened? She could almost believe in love at first sight, in fate and all the crap she'd previously scoffed at.

God, I've got it so bad.

She rummaged through the freezer and found some frozen chicken breasts and a bag of vegetables. She set to work on supper. She didn't know what time he'd be home, but she was starving and cooking would occupy her mind.

She filled a pan with the vegetables and the chicken, a can of chopped tomatoes and seasoned them with salt and pepper. Someone must have stocked the cottage before they'd come. No way would all this stuff be edible after months, even in the coldness of the fridge and freezer. The heady scent of the food cooking permeated the basement in no time at all, and, with no choice left, at eleven p.m. she settled down to read a book she'd found lying around — an old-style romance, one of those bodice-ripper books. What the hell was that doing here? Did the people who used this cottage regularly bring women here?

The book pissed her off. She couldn't for the life of her think how the woman in it could fall for a hero who was so fucking cruel. After some time she put the book down and pondered on the similarities between the hero and Bishop. *He* could be seen as cruel — a kidnapper, someone who'd gripped her up in the bathroom of the previous hideout, a man who'd fucked her as soon as she'd offered it.

But he isn't. I know it. There's someone kind underneath.

She forced the flashing neon words in her mind away, the ones saying, *You're a fool if you think you can snare him for good.* She went to check on the casserole, lifting the lid. The scents were amazing. Some of the smaller potatoes had disintegrated to thicken the intense tomato sauce while some larger ones had kept their shape. As she tasted the warm liquid, she closed her eyes. She could really cook. Would that be a plus for her?

The way to a man's heart…

Fallan began to serve the meal on two plates, making sure Bishop got a good amount of chicken. The sound of the lift door opening then closing made her turn to look. Bishop walked to the kitchen area, his complexion pale. She knew he'd killed someone again, but instead of questioning him on his business, she smiled and held a plate towards him.

"Just in time for dinner," she said.

He relaxed a little and took the plate from her. "I didn't know you could cook."

"There's a lot you don't know about me."

On her venture around the basement earlier she'd located a bottle of white wine and now brought it with her to the table. Glasses were on the counter, and, as Bishop tucked into his meal, she poured some wine and sat opposite him.

"What have you done this evening?" he asked.

It was on the tip of her tongue to ask what exactly *he'd* done but she held it in. Being insensitive would get her nowhere. He hadn't wanted to kill.

"Don't laugh, but I cleaned up the mess in the bedroom and made dinner. Read a very strange and bizarre story about a woman who falls for the guy who forced himself on her. Then I served dinner and you came home. That's it, the sum of my evening."

Bishop laughed. "I know the book you mean."

They ate in silence, but not an uncomfortable one. Fallan could easily get used to this. Him going to 'work' and coming home. Them acting like a couple.

Am I crazy wanting him even though I know he's now a killer?

She might be, but it didn't seem to matter. Once they were done eating, she cleared away the dishes and spent time washing them, the sides and the cooker. Only when everything was completed did she go into the sitting room area. Bishop came out of the office and sat in the chair, an alcoholic drink in hand.

"Cameras are off," he said. "I thought that might be a good idea seeing as you're naked. Relax."

She watched him sip his drink for a moment, wondering whether she ought to strike up a conversation or let him lead.

"You know," he said, solving the problem for her, "when I went to work for the government, I thought I'd be on protective detail or something like that. I'm one hell of a bodyguard and would give my life to save someone of importance."

Fallan sat in one corner of the sofa and waited for him to continue. Her speaking might break the spell he appeared to be in. He stared at the floor, seeing things she couldn't—images in his head that had no business being there, possibly of the men he'd killed. How did that affect a person? How did not having any choice make him feel? She longed to ask but didn't dare. He might clam up and refuse to speak about it again. She needed to know more about him, for them to grow closer. Now that the dangerous men had been removed from the equation, it stood to reason she'd be taken home, never to see him again. She didn't want that to happen—wanted to share some feelings with him before then so she made some kind of impact other than being a woman he'd fucked for fun.

He sighed. "It wasn't long until Huntington pulled me away from the mundane jobs. Everything was going fine before that. Small details like escorting someone to a special hideout, to locating missing evidence, shit like that. I didn't sign up for *this*. I signed up to take the bullet, not shoot one in someone's head."

"Is that what you did today?" she asked quietly.

He chuckled. "While you were making a delicious meal fit for any king, I was busy putting a bullet through a bad guy's skull. Why? Huntington's way of teaching me a lesson, I think. I swear to you I never wanted to kill anyone, and knowing I have makes me feel like the worst scum in the world."

Fallan thought through what he'd said. She should be terrified, but seeing the look of shock and fear in his face she knew he was horrified by what he'd done.

"At least you killed bad guys," she said, trying to soothe the hurt.

She suspected he'd push her away if she went to embrace him. Bishop needed to get this off his chest, not worry about some woman pawing at him.

"I know, but how do I know that underneath they weren't just like me? Men who got where they were out of necessity rather than choosing? How do I know anything anymore?" He got up and went to stare at a large canvas of Brooklyn Bridge on the wall opposite his chair.

She went over to him and placed a hand on his shoulder. "When my mother died I didn't know what I was going to do. I was suddenly alone in the world with no hope, you know? You might think I'm greedy for wanting to take that money and that I'm a whore for negotiating the money for our time together, but it isn't like that. As people we get desperate. When a way out presents itself, sometimes we have to take it no matter how bad it is. I mean, look at me as an example. I have to have that ten grand to pay off debts. If fucking you helped me get it, then I knew that's what I'd have to do, but now? It's...different."

"What do you mean?" He continued to stare ahead.

"It doesn't matter. You don't need to hear the shit going on in my head."

"Maybe I want to."

"And maybe you're just saying that so you don't have to focus on the shit in yours."

"Indulge me."

She took a deep breath. He meant something to her, and if she had to make a fool of herself to let him know, face rejection, then at least she'd tried. "It's different because... Fuck, all right, I'll be blunt, seeing as that's how I've been with you from the start. I like you, okay? At first it *was* just a fuck, but something happened, something clicked, and now I want to see more of you—outside of this weird-arse situation. I might be mad for that, but I don't care."

"I see." He blinked several times.

"Listen," she said, "you're good at what you do and I know deep down you understand this person you killed had to go." She turned him to face her and cupped his cheek. "Please, don't let this turn you into something you're not."

"How can you be so sure I'm not the bad guy?"

He stared into her eyes and for a second laid everything bare. She saw his pain, his dilemma, the way his mind was working to justify what he'd done. The way he'd failed to come up with an adequate answer that would remove the guilt.

"You could've killed me but you didn't." Fallan stopped herself from saying anything more. She wanted to tell him she loved him, but how could she, after only spending hours with him? What the fuck had happened here? She knew with all of her heart and soul she loved this strange and unusual man, time issue be damned.

Fallan couldn't break their gaze. Bishop leant down and kissed her. Emotions instant and hot, she melted against him.

The world and her life didn't matter when she was in his arms.

He pulled back from her lips. "I want you," he whispered. "God fucking help me, and I don't understand it, but this isn't just a fuck for me, either. It's... Christ, it's like you said. Different."

"Then have me." She stroked the hair at the back of his neck and laid little kisses along his cheek and neck.

"My job isn't one I can get out of now—probably couldn't before today, either. You'd have to keep secrets, keep our real life hidden from everyone you know. If we got together..." He shook his head. "It isn't possible. It isn't fair to you."

"I don't care." Fallan didn't want to analyse his comments. It wasn't for her to judge. What he did just didn't seem to matter, and maybe one day she'd look back and see all this crazy for what it was, but at the moment... No, she'd go with her gut. She wanted this. Him.

Bishop wrapped his arms more tightly around her and slowly walked her back through the basement until she landed sitting on the bed. She watched him strip and reveal the expanse of wonderful male flesh. His body was gorgeous. She wanted to lick every inch of him. Naked, he grasped her hand and pulled her to stand, then kissed her while hugging her bare flesh to him. In no time they were doing nothing but making love with their lips, his cock digging into her stomach. She reached down to hold the hard, thick length of him. His essence leaked out of the tip and she used it as an aid to masturbate him. Bishop groaned and slowly pushed her until she lay back on the sheets.

Fallan opened her legs and smiled.

"I shouldn't do this," he muttered, hovering over her and grazing her lips with his.

"Why? I'm a willing woman and I want to be here. I want to be with you."

He shook his head. "One last time. I can enjoy you one last time."

He kissed her long and deep, as though conveying how much he cared for her, but she shoved that thought away. She'd fallen for him, not the other way around, and thinking he gave a shit was dangerous. She wanted to stop the kiss and ask '*What do you mean, one last time?*' She didn't want this to end, for this to be it. She wanted to be with him for the rest of her life.

Bishop circled her breasts, pulling one nipple to attention. She moaned as he kissed her and loved each of her mounds in turn, devoting extra attention to each the longer he caressed. She couldn't bear it. The attention and the way he was behaving... She knew this was their last time together, knew she should enjoy it so she'd know she'd given him the best fuck he'd ever had, but emotions were getting in the way. Insistent questions ricocheted through her mind.

How can I let this be the last time? How will anyone match up to him? Why has he affected me like this when no one else ever has? What is it about him that has me willing to give up everything?

How can I let him walk away when he takes me back home, knowing I'll never see him again?

Whomever he'd killed today had been the person who'd posed a threat to her. He'd done his job, she'd get paid, life would return to the boring normality it had been before she'd found herself at a hotel then been swept away by this man who suckled her nipples and sent her libido soaring.

Their situation was unfair. They hadn't had enough time.

She loved Bishop, or was seriously on the way to it, and love was supposed to conquer all, not leave a horrible void in one's chest.

She blanked out every thought and horrid feeling — she didn't want to spend her last time hating him for leaving her. Instead, she opened her heart and loved him with all the passion and desire she could. No matter what happened next, she'd always have her memories of him. They would have to do.

She stroked his back as he moved down her body, kissing her stomach then down to her pussy. She'd always be ready to take him. Cream wet her slit. She allowed the sensation of him licking her cunt to override everything else. She gasped and arched up to meet every lick and thrust of his tongue. Reaching up to the headboard, she held on as an orgasm washed over her, causing her to scream out in absolute blinding pleasure.

Not done with her, he climbed up and kissed her, plunging his tongue inside her mouth. Her taste exploded on her tongue and she moaned. So erotic and naughty, but with Bishop she wanted more. Always more.

He placed one hand between them and grasped his cock, aligning his tip with her entrance. He glided into her soaked folds tantalisingly slowly.

"I want to last," he moaned as he slid all the way inside her to the hilt. "But I don't think I can. Fuck, you do something to me, woman."

Full to the brim, Fallan wrapped her arms around his neck and he began a rhythm that would take her to the stars. He pulled her legs high on his waist and fucked her, never breaking contact with her lips. They kissed throughout. The man in her arms wasn't a killer but a man desperate for love. Bishop would have her love for the rest of his life whether she was in it or not. Anything and everything he wanted she'd give, if only he'd let her.

He climaxed, crying her name, and another, soft-yet-sweet orgasm took hold of her. She shuddered with him, shifting one hand to the back of his head so she could kiss him deeper. He slowed to a stop and broke his mouth from hers, and they lay in each other's arms. They didn't have to speak—she was just content they were together.

Throughout the night he made love to her repeatedly, his thrusts slow, and drew out every last ounce of pleasure she had left. Fallan stayed in his arms, never wanting to let go.

She knew come morning it would all end, the wonderful future she'd envisaged nothing but a pipe dream.

And Bishop would become nothing more than a memory.

Chapter Thirteen

Once again, Bishop woke to the sound of the telephone rudely intruding on his time with Fallan. She stirred but didn't wake. More reluctant than ever to leave their warm nest in bed, he got out with the urge to rail against the world and everyone in it. Life had suddenly got very unfair. Quickly going to the office and closing the door, he picked up the receiver.

"What," he said, irritated that Huntington wanted him so early in the goddamn morning.

"Good morning, Bishop. A little testy today?"

"What do you want?"

"It's time to ship her home."

"What, now?" He glanced at the clock on the wall. "It's only six, for fuck's sake."

"Best time to do it. Hardly anyone about when you drop her off. Less chance of you being seen."

"Can't it wait until tonight? Usually after a job I have downtime. This is it."

"But you can't have downtime when the job isn't complete. To complete it you need to take Miss Jones home."

Fuck. "I need time to prepare her. Need to let her know she has to keep her mouth shut. Make her understand."

"I rather think she understands already, Bishop, don't you?"

Bishop sighed. Of course she did. Him killing had seen to that. "I want to wait until tonight. I don't ask for much, never go against your wishes, but I will now. I'd prefer to do so with your consent, though. A few more hours, that's all I want."

"My, my, the little woman really has affected you, hasn't she?"

"If you say so. I'm more concerned that she returns to her life with her mental health intact. She's been through a lot. We can't just dump her after what's happened and expect her to carry on as normal. She isn't like the other women on this scam. They weren't aware of things Fallan now knows. They have no idea about the government involvement. At present, I'd say Fallan poses a risk."

"In what way?"

"She's vulnerable. What if she needs someone to talk to?"

"Like the other women?"

"What do you mean?"

"They returned home last night to find their money in their homes — courtesy of us, of course — then went on to telephone, despite Frankie Lash's warnings not to, every friend they have with news of their windfall and how they got it."

"Shit."

"Indeed."

"What's the next step regarding them?"

"The next step has already been taken by the agent you saw outside Lash's flat. While you slept, he was rather busy."

Bishop's stomach rolled. "What have you done?"

"They're all dead, Bishop."

"What?" His head lightened and his knees buckled. Bile surged into his throat, and he swallowed, wincing at the burn. "You're serious, aren't you?"

"When am I ever not? They were a threat. They knew the information in those bags was important enough that they had to remain silent, yet they chose not to heed Lash's warning. Excitement at receiving the money had obviously addled their minds."

Bishop latched on to that. "All the more reason for me to make sure Fa — Miss Jones doesn't fall into the same trap. I don't want her killed, Huntington."

"I'm sure you don't. But your dick is currently doing the talking here, Bishop. Do not lose sight of the job and what you're employed to do."

"So I get to keep her until tonight?"

"Yes, but that's it. Tell her the score — make sure she understands fully. Tell her about the other women if you have to, but she needs to be returned home before someone misses her."

"As opposed to someone missing her after you've had her killed? What's the fucking difference?"

Huntington sighed. "The difference is quite simple. Her not being at home or work when she should be, and no one knowing where she is, brings the police into the equation — questions will need to be answered, trails followed... You get the idea. Worried people tend to call the police when someone doesn't show up for an extended period. Her being at home, dead, found by someone who called on her to see why she wasn't at work, or called the police after her phone went unanswered, solves any problems. She's in sight, albeit murdered—or maybe we'll make it look like a suicide, who knows?—and it's the better option. Questions answered, T's crossed, I's dotted."

"Christ, you're so...so fucking blasé about this shit."

"I have to be. It's my job. Just like it should be yours. You should never have got involved with her."

I know, but I couldn't fucking help myself...

"Tonight, Bishop. After eleven p.m. No later, understand?"

"Yes."

"And make sure she's aware of the consequences. No soft-soaping. If you care for her as much as I suspect, you'll need to be cruel to be kind. Scare her and scare her well."

"I will."

"Right, well, make sure you do, otherwise, if she calls someone and explains what she's been doing, her blood is on your hands."

Bishop slammed the phone into the cradle. It was just like Huntington to shift the damn blame. Maybe that was how the man coped with what he had to do, but Bishop wanted none of this bollocks anymore. If he had the balls he'd leave, take all his fake passports and disappear, but what was the point? The government had issued those passports, would be looking for him within a second of him not reporting in when he should. Would even be watching him as he prepared to scarper. He was stuck. A rock and a fucking hard place had never been so true.

He braced himself on the desk, hanging his head and closing his eyes. After a few deep breaths, he sat in the chair and leant back, preparing to sort through the muddle his mind had become. He'd have to let her go for her own good. There was no way Huntington would allow him to continue seeing her. The web they weaved would grow more intricate, each tendril stretching to the next, a seemingly faultless vision that was far from the illusion it gave. It might be pretty to look at, but those perfectly formed rectangles each held hidden dangers for Fallan. She'd be walking their delicate strands like a tightrope, trying not to fall through the spaces into oblivion below — Huntington, the hulking spider in the centre, watching her fall and not mourning her as a lost meal.

She was expendable, and Bishop hated that fact.

He rose and returned to the bedroom, standing against the doorjamb and watching her sleep. Although she was beautiful to look at, he sensed that beauty extended inside her, a woman who, despite her brash exterior, had a soft centre and so much to give the right man. Much as he wished that right man were him, he had to face the truth. In another time, another place, another damn world, he *was* that man, but in this one? No. She deserved better than he could give. What woman deserved a life like the one she'd have if he dragged her along with him? How could he live knowing she knew he did horrendous things and expect her to keep those secrets? He'd be giving her a heavy burden to carry, and, because he'd begun to care about her, that wasn't something he was prepared to do. If you loved someone, you didn't cause them pain. Yes, he'd be giving her a massive dose of it when it came time for them to part, but time would erase him, and, if it didn't, it would at least dull the edges of her memories so he wasn't as stark in her mind and heart. This was how it had to be. She could move on and meet someone else, have a new man to keep her from remembering Bishop.

The thought of that hurt more than he'd believed possible. Another man touching her, seeing her smile, being with her every day…

Fuck, it should be me. I want it to be me.

He readied himself for the last hours in her company by inhaling deeply then exhaling with force. Today had to count. Memories had to be made.

Ones that would last a lifetime for both of them.

* * * *

They spent the day as any other new couple, laughing, talking, telling one another a little of their pasts. Bishop soaked up every word she said, filing it away for later down the line when he had time on his hands between jobs and needed to remember. He wouldn't be with any other woman, not like this. Yes, he was a realist and knew he'd fuck, but that's all it would be. No emotions, no sentiment, just a release of sexual tension.

He studied everything about her. The way she moved. How she raised her eyebrows and widened her eyes before laughter took hold of her. The tilt of her head and narrowing of her eyes when they discussed something painful from their pasts. How she took his hand and everything bad melted away at her touch. Remaining in the basement with her forever was an appealing concept—and, by God, he wished they could do that—but life had other ideas, *people* had other ideas, and in the end life was governed not by what one wanted but by outside influences.

Fate was a cruel bitch sometimes.

By dinnertime, he kept glancing at the clock, torturing himself by counting how many minutes they had left. Minutes looked more plentiful as opposed to hours—gave the illusion that extra time was available. For a few seconds he kidded himself, as she had him stirring the tagliatelle in the pan, that this was how it would always be—they'd cook together after a long day at work, eat at a table with several candles, then snuggle on the sofa watching, but not really watching, some boring crap on TV. Talking, sharing experiences. Being.

She glanced up at him while stirring her own pot— the carbonara she'd miraculously created out of nowhere—and, shit, his heart literally ached. A void grew in his chest, one hell of a gaping hole that left him breathless and with the urge to lash out. He stifled it, pushed it the fuck away—there was plenty of time ahead to investigate that hole when she was no longer around.

They ate as though on a first date, him holding out her chair before she sat, serving the food, treating her like the princess she'd become throughout the day. She was hurting too, he could see it, but she was a good actress. Anyone watching—and they weren't, he'd kept those bastard cameras turned off—would naturally assume she was a happy woman.

After they'd cleared up, he led her to the sofa and put the TV on, wanting what he'd thought of earlier — a semblance of them being a couple. It worked for a while, the pretending, the make-believe scenario they both wanted but hadn't voiced, but, after an hour of the TV being on and them ignoring it, talking and holding hands, kissing and losing themselves in one another, the time had come for Bishop to give Fallan a lesson he'd been putting off all day.

Reality 101.

If she listened attentively and fully understood everything he had to say, he could give her a pass — an A plus.

"Fallan, I —"

"I don't want to hear it." She bit her lower lip.

"I know, and I don't want to say it but I have to."

"Fuck." She traced circles on the back of his hand with her thumb.

"There are some things you have to know before I take you home."

"I don't want to go home."

She pouted, mirroring his feelings exactly.

"I don't want to take you home. I want... I wish..." He couldn't do this to her. Couldn't say what he really wanted.

"You wish what? Please, tell me. If you've got feelings for me I want to know. It'll make this easier."

Would it, though? He wasn't so sure about that. Still, if that was what she wanted. He'd discovered today he couldn't deny her a goddamn thing. "I wish we could stay here. I wish I didn't have the job I have, even though me having it meant I met you. I wish I could rewind time and change it so you'd just taken a normal weekend break and so had I. That we'd met in the dining room and... But we didn't. No point in wishing otherwise. Even if we had met like that it would still be a risk having you in my life. Even though you know what my job entails, if we'd met another way I wouldn't have been able to tell you much. You'd always have wondered what I did that had to be such a secret. It'd have created tension. You'd have been left worrying what I was up to, whether I was really seeing other women when I worked odd hours and fucked off at a moment's notice. Maybe we wouldn't have worked..."

She squeezed his hand and rested her head on his shoulder. "But I *do* know. And it doesn't bother me. It should, I realise that, and I know maybe I'm mad or blinded by you enough that what you do doesn't matter, but, if being with you means knowing you kill people, I'll deal with it."

"I can't ask you to do that." He kissed the top of her head.

"You wouldn't be asking. I want to."

"But I can't be with you, don't you understand?"

She lifted her head and stared at him. "Yes, I understand that Huntington pulls the damn strings, that he's the one determining what the fuck I do with my life, what you do with yours. Yes, I understand, and it fucking stinks, all right? I'm an adult, I should be able to do whatever the hell I want, and having some government arsehole dictating how I live and stopping me being with the man I lo—like a lot— pisses me the hell off. Why can't he see I won't say anything? Why can't you tell him I'll keep my mouth shut? I swear to God I will."

"Because people always say that until things go wrong."

"But we wouldn't *go* wrong! I *know* we wouldn't."

"I know what you're saying. I feel the same right now, but we're at the start of something, so of course everything seems all right, of course we'd swear we were going to last forever, but shit happens, life happens, and, if we ever had to part ways, you'd be a massive liability to the government. You could open your mouth, tell the wrong people all the information you know, and—"

"But I wouldn't. I'm not like that!"

"I have a feeling you're telling the truth, but Huntington doesn't see it that way. He has to cover all bases, you see? This is the government we're talking about, a massive organisation where one wrong word can cause shitloads of trouble. You might not even mean to say anything, but words have a habit of slipping out and —"

"So you're saying I can't be trusted because I might blab something by accident, is that it?"

The pain in her eyes tore at him. Yes, that's exactly what he'd said, no getting away from it. "It happens, Fallan. I'm a realist. Much as I'd love to be a dreamer with you, I can't be."

"What if I sign something? Get that Huntington fucker here right now and have me sign for silence. I just want to be with you." She gripped him tight around the waist and squeezed. "I sound like a bloody whiny female, needy and all that crap, but this is my life, my *feelings* here. I don't know how this happened between us, how I feel like this, but I do, and trying to turn it off... It's going to *hurt,* damn it!" She jumped up and paced, fists bunched. "Fuck this shit! Where's the phone? I want to speak to that bastard."

"That isn't a good idea, Fallan."

"Neither is us being parted when we don't want to be."

He eyed her, noting her determination to get what she wanted. "You might not hear what you want to hear."

"I know that," she said, flashing him a blazing look, "but I have to know I tried everything. If I don't, I'll beat myself up with more regrets than I already have."

"All right, but he'll tell you things...things I should have told you by now."

"Then let him tell me. Let *him* have the burden of having to explain."

Gritting his teeth to ward off the wave of emotion rising inside him, Bishop stood and led her to the office. He thought of everything he hadn't told her and, as he dialled, imagined how Huntington would give the information. Blunt. To the point. Harsh.

"Yes, Bishop? Are you done with your little talk?"

"Uh, no. I didn't get that far yet."

"Putting it off, are we?"

"No, I went to explain the facts but—"

"Give me that damn phone," Fallan said. She held out her hand, cheeks red, mouth pursed.

"Miss Jones would like to hear it from you," Bishop said, clutching the receiver tight to his ear.

"Very well. Put her on."

Bishop pressed the speakerphone button. "Go ahead." He nodded at Fallan.

"What the fuck is wrong with you?" she said to the phone, leaning over it with her hands on the desk. "I mean, I have a situation here I didn't expect to be in, and now I'm in it I don't want to get out. I don't care about the bollocks that got me here, understand? I don't give a shit what you lot get up to, how you earn your wages. I just want to be able to see Bishop."

"I'm afraid that isn't possible, Miss Jones," Huntington said.

"Why the fuck not?" she yelled.

Huntington cleared his throat. "Do you value your life, Miss Jones?"

"Of course I bloody do," she snapped, launching off the desk to pace. "What kind of stupid question is that?" She paused, then said, "Oh, was that a *threat*?"

"Yes. If you value your life—and Bishop's—you'll return home and keep everything you've learned to yourself."

"Oh," she said, some of the bluster gone from her voice. "Are you saying that if I don't return to my usual life and forget about Bishop he'll be in danger from the people who employ him? The people who he works to protect? Fucking charming." She narrowed her eyes and bared her teeth. "Answer me!"

"Yes, that is correct, Miss Jones."

She stared at Bishop, eyes filling, throat bobbing. "Then you have my silence."

"I thought I might. You will be watched, Miss Jones. Any contact with Bishop is strictly prohibited. Any information you have learned from this mission is not to be repeated to anyone. If we find out you've broken this agreement—"

"Yes, I understand. I'll be terminated, or whatever the hell you like to call it to make yourself feel better."

"Are you aware about the other women, Miss Jones?"

"What about them?" She widened her eyes at Bishop and held her hands up in a what-the-fuck gesture.

"They're all dead."

Bishop watched the colour drain from her face. She staggered towards the chair behind the desk and flopped into it.

"Why?" she asked quietly.

"They talked."

"Shit."

"Yes, quite. So you understand?"

"Yes," she whispered.

"Good. Prepare yourself to leave the location."

The call was severed, much like Bishop's tie to Fallan would be in an hour or so.

He couldn't look at her, couldn't bear to see the tears fall, but he heard her sobs.

The worst sound of his goddamn, shitty little life.

Chapter Fourteen

Bishop pulled up outside Fallan's house. His nerves pinged more than they did when he was on a mission. His heart beat erratically, and he stared across at her in the van's passenger seat, wishing with everything he had in him that things could be different. They couldn't—he had to say goodbye—but a few more minutes in her company wouldn't hurt.

"You can take the blindfold off now," he said, failing to keep his voice steady.

She bent her head then sat still, as though delaying the inevitable. He understood how she felt completely. If she was going through what he was, her heart was being twisted and her emotions had turned sour, scoring her insides, their path reaching her soul with spiteful accuracy. By fuck, this hurt more than he'd imagined, and a lump formed in his throat. Damned if he would cry, though.

That could come later, after he'd swallowed the last drop from a bottle of whisky.

She reached up a shaking hand and drew the blindfold off, turning to him with glistening eyes and a downturned, quivering mouth. He wanted to kiss it all away — this horror, this miasma of gut-wrenching feelings that threatened to overwhelm them both — but he had a job to conclude, lives to save. His and Fallan's.

"So this is it, then?" she said, the words so quiet they were barely there. "This is how it ends. We say goodbye in a van. I get out, don't look back, and have to continue with my life as though none of this ever happened."

He nodded. "Something like that."

"I hate this," she whispered, one tear spilling, reaching her jaw line then dripping off onto a grey T-shirt from the basement wardrobe.

"Me too."

"And it feels awkward, like I don't know you. Like we never —"

"I know. Perhaps it's better this way. Perhaps we ought to just cut ties quickly and pretend we never met."

"Maybe." She clamped her lips closed, but they quivered some more, and it was clear she was struggling to keep them still.

"Fallan, I —"

"It's okay." She waved at him dismissively. "Shit happens." She smoothed down her hair. "Story of my fucking life. I should be used to it by now." She attempted a wobbly smile but it looked more like a grimace. "Still, I'd rather this than him *terminating* you. At least we can still dream. I'll think of you, you'll think of me, and we'll get a few smiles out of it. Memories will fade and all that rubbish. Time heals. We'll move on."

"We will." *I don't want to.*

"So!" she said on an exhale, smiling over-brightly. "Give me that last kiss and I'll be gone. Mission complete. Secrets are safe."

"Not here," he said. "I have to see you inside."

"Ah, make sure nothing weird has been planted in my house, that it? Make sure Waterman or Frankie Lash didn't leave me any nasty surprises."

He nodded. "Better to be safe than sorry."

"Oh, I'm already damn well sorry." She yanked at the door handle and left the van, her movements jerky, shoulders a rigid, straight line.

He admired her strength, her determination to see this through with dignity. She closed her door and walked around to his, and waited there on the pavement, a magnolia bush and blackthorn tree behind her. He took in that sight for a moment, her framed by foliage darkened by the night, her face white and pinched, hands by her sides, clenching in and out of fists. She stared through the window at him, and he wondered what was going through her mind. Was she imprinting his image there as he was with her? Was she battling with a lump in her throat so big it almost cut off her air supply? Was she thinking *I wish, I wish, I wish*…?

He couldn't *think* anymore so got out of the van and locked it, then led the way to her house. An envelope had been wedged between the house and an empty terracotta plant pot, and he stooped to pick it up. Opened it. Read the contents. Reached up to the eaves in the porch overhang and found a set of keys.

He turned to look at her behind him. "Your locks have been changed."

"Okay," she said, lifting her chin.

He unlocked the door and went inside, holding one finger to his lips and miming that he wanted her to stand beside the closed door and wait. He switched on the lights as he went, checking every room, behind and under furniture, looking for planted bugs and finding several. He left them in place—they were for her own good.

Back in the hallway, he said, "To guarantee your silence, your place has been bugged."

She stood straighter. "The bugs aren't needed. I won't be telling anyone *anything*."

"I know that, but Huntington—"

"Is a prick who has to be in control of everything." She sighed. "Yes, I understand why, understand it all, but it doesn't mean I have to like it."

"No. Me neither." He couldn't look at her, so focused his attention on a small window beside the front door. A tall blue vase held a variety of wooden swirls and fake flowers, and either side of that two crystal keys sat on intricately carved bases.

She laughed bitterly. "I bought those thinking that one day I'd have that, you know? Two keys to my home and life instead of just mine. Turns out I do...but then again I don't." She reached out and picked one up. "Here, take it."

He accepted the gift, the crystal cold on his palm, and smiled just as bitterly as she'd laughed. Crystal was apt. Unfeeling. Hard. "Thank you," he managed and slipped it into his pocket.

He moved closer to her, lifting his arm to settle one finger beneath her chin. He ducked his head, touching his mouth to hers, dipping his tongue inside.

She tasted of broken dreams.

Tears blinding him, he drew away from her and opened the door. With his back to her, he said, "Your money is on the kitchen table."

"Thank you," she said.

"I'll never forget you, Fallan. *Never*."

He walked down the path, wanting to turn around, wanting to crush her to him and smell her scent, feel her heart thumping, wipe away the tears he knew were there because her sobs punctuated his every step. To tell her he'd take care of her from the outside, that he'd make sure she never came to any harm. That loving her from afar was all he could give. That he wished her well in the arms of another man, in another life filled with nothing but happiness.

But he didn't.

Fallan watched him leave. She stood and let him go, knowing in her heart if she went after him Huntington would kill him. New tears wouldn't fall till much later. She walked through her house and noted nothing had changed in her absence. It still smelt clean and every item had a place to sit. The scent of vanilla hung in the air from the polish she liked to use.

Polish? She was thinking of a type of cleaner at a time like this?

It felt as though her heart had just been ripped out of her chest and squashed, and she was thinking about stupid fucking shit that didn't have any importance in the scheme of things.

She thought about her time with Bishop, and the anger at her situation overrode common sense. Fallan lashed out. She tore down pictures from walls and smashed ornaments. No surface and nothing was safe from her pain. He'd left her without a fight. Yes, she was fully aware of why he'd let her go, but it still stung like hell. She could never have him and it hurt more than anything in the world. With her mother she'd had the chance to say goodbye properly. She'd been ready for the loss of her parents, but not Bishop. She'd had the most amazing days spent in his company, in his arms, and now she had nothing.

Time would come and go and the memories would fade to be nothing more than a passing whisper. But could she live knowing Bishop was the love of her life and she'd never see him again?

Why was the world being unfair to her once again?

She stared at the chaos around her, caused by her own hands. There would be no magical cure for her broken heart. With tears streaming down her face, she went into the kitchen and gathered a dustpan and brush along with the vacuum cleaner. For the next hour she poured her heart and soul into cleaning. She picked through the pictures of her parents along with ones of her as she'd grown up, careful to not cut her fingers on the shards of glass.

Once the mess was cleaned and the broken glass placed in a bag for recycling she went back into her kitchen and put the kettle on. She sat at the table and saw a thick white envelope resting on the surface. Fallan reached out and grabbed it, tearing it open. Inside was the ten grand she'd been promised but also a debit card. Frowning, she pulled all the contents out. She pushed the money away, wanting nothing to do with the stuff, realising how crazy that was when she'd done all this for that very money in the first place. She'd rather be with Bishop than have the money.

The debit card didn't make any sense and with it came a note. Before she opened and read its contents, she made herself a strong coffee and did something she'd never done before—she added a huge amount of brandy to her cup. The cheap stuff, but it would still give her the desired effect. Right now she needed the numbness cheap booze could supply. Instead of putting the bottle away, she placed it next to the money and flipped open the letter.

Dear Fallan,

I've left ten thousand pounds on the table. I know writing it all out seems very formal, but you're a devil for keeping quiet when I'm talking so at least this way I get to say what I have to. As I write this you're sleeping in the bed in the basement apartment. You look so beautiful. I've never felt like this before in my life and, as you can probably tell, I've never written a proper letter to a woman either. I'm useless at both—having feelings, writing.

So, here's the gist of it, things you probably know by now. Huntington has demanded I leave you otherwise there will be a threat to your life and mine. I think we know I couldn't kill you even if I was told to, but I wouldn't put it past the arsehole to make me be the one to do it if I broke my promise to stay away. At the point of writing this I haven't told you how I feel and I guess I'm doing this so you'll know what you mean to me if something happens to me. The truth is, Fallan Jones, checkout girl at Asda, you own my heart. I'm completely, absolutely in love with you.

It will grieve me more than anything leaving you. I've sorted some things out for you. In this world I want nothing more than to know you're happy, so your house is paid in full along with all of your other debts. You can take the money and do what you want. I've also set you up an account so you can live well and do whatever you want without financial worry.

This is my way of taking care of you the best way I know how. I love you, my darling Fallan, and know for the rest of my life my heart will be only yours.

Bishop.

P.S. Please don't bin the card or the money. The PIN is 8572. You deserve something good in this life. Please let me be the one responsible for giving it to you.

She sobbed. Long and hard. Body-jerking and harsh. She ignored the coffee and went straight for the bottle of brandy. The bitter taste and acrid burn did nothing to stop the tears falling even more. She wanted to be brave and throw everything away. The money, the card and demand for the house to be unpaid. Another swig from the bottle and she reread the letter. Bishop loved her and she loved him. Why couldn't they be together?

Fallan understood why but the reasoning behind it seemed so fucked up and stupid. She had nothing waiting in the future for her. If Fallan Jones walked off the face of the earth, the only people who'd care would be the government because of the possible tax earning on the money she left behind. Bishop's money.

She thought about her time with him. At the initial meeting he'd been so masculine, taking charge like that. She'd been scared and excited. Bishop was a gorgeous man and she'd responded to that.

When had her feelings gone from being simply lust to love? She couldn't remember the exact moment. Was it during sex? They'd had so much of it in the short time they'd known each other but she wouldn't have had it any other way. Bishop had cared for her and learnt every detail he could from his little computer.

She'd shocked him several times, though. Fallan smiled as she recalled how she'd surprised him when she'd taken him in her mouth. The way she'd turned into his submissive. All of the new memories she'd created for him. She took the brandy bottle and walked upstairs to her room. The double bed was a welcome sight and she flopped down face first, some of the brandy spilling out and wetting her and the bed. Moaning, she rolled over and looked at the light above the bed.

The perv, Huntington, was probably watching her or listening.

"See, you bastard, I've done nothing and I've got nowhere to go—no one to tell this shit to!" she shouted up at the light. She threw some of the brandy and laughed at herself when it splashed all over her instead. There was no one to enjoy her pity party with. Only some weirdo government official on the other end of an intrusive camera.

It wasn't fair. Love was supposed to conquer everything and she had nothing to conquer anymore. The only reason she couldn't be with Bishop was because of his job description. She had fuck all left— no parent, siblings, and nothing to hold her back from going for what she wanted.

But what did she want?

Fallan ran downstairs, swiping her face, then opened her front door. She gazed out at the dark street and glanced around, checking for signs of people watching her home. Her body clock was out of whack. She was pleased she lived in a detached house otherwise the neighbours would have called out about the disturbance earlier.

No more what ifs. No more wallowing in self-pity. She refused to go through this life only ever knowing what love could be like if they'd only had the chance to make a good go of it. She wanted Bishop and no one was going to tell her she couldn't have him. Where there was a will there was a way.

She returned to her bedroom, packed a bag and thought about a plan that had formed from nowhere. Huntington had said Bishop was at risk if she was a citizen in his life, someone who might give up agency secrets, tire of him constantly being away on assignment. If Bishop couldn't be with her then maybe, just maybe, there was another way.

She hated being told what to do. Hated the thought of not being allowed to spend her life with Bishop. Determined to get what she wanted, she picked up the phone and made a call that would change everything.

Chapter Fifteen

Six months later

Bishop's career was all he had left, and making sure he did everything to the letter was the only way he could keep Fallan safe. During the first month after they'd parted, while working he'd remained focused on the mission—it had included killing someone—but when he'd had time to himself he'd filled it with thoughts of her. She visited him in his dreams, her scent wafting around him, her smile sad, her whispered endearments mirroring his feelings for her. Once, when he'd woken in a sweat and called out her name, he'd entertained the thought that they were connected, that she was reaching out to him through thoughts and dreams, but that was just wishful thinking. Shit like that couldn't happen. Didn't happen. It helped him to cope, though, and, as mad as it sounded, if he imagined her aching for him like he did for her, life wasn't so bad.

Maybe in the next one they'd get to be together.

Huntington gave him monthly reports on her, and the days in between them dragged. He lived for when he'd get an update, and, although he should want her to be happy, when he was told she appeared to be living but not *living*, that she had dark circles beneath her eyes and rarely smiled, he felt a guilty twinge of satisfaction. It was natural not to want her finding solace with someone else, yet he'd berated himself too many times to count that he was supposed to love her, so having her happy should be the top of his wish list.

It wasn't, and he hated himself for it.

His last job had been a tough one. Now it was over, he had two weeks of downtime in which to indulge himself. With a set of headphones on, he rested on his sofa, feet propped on the arm, and let the harmonies lull him into that place where he wasn't awake or asleep. Where he was in limbo.

Fallan danced, her smile bright, arms lifted to take him into a comforting embrace. He saw every detail of her as though she really stood before him, and for a few seconds he believed he was there with her. A change in the music's tempo brought him out of his dream state and she disappeared, leaving him feeling as he had on the night he'd taken her back home.

Bereft. Alone. Broken.

Eyes closed, he reached into his pocket, feeling for the crystal key. He pulled it out then enclosed his fist around it. Did she do the same with the other one, or did it still sit on the windowsill beside her front door? Holding the key brought him closer to her, as though it had been infused with her essence—another of his imaginings. He'd become a romantic sap since their parting—dreaming, wishing, hoping that things could have been different. If those he'd killed only knew how he really felt inside...

A sudden and sharp longing gripped him—one where he wanted to hear her voice, to see her. It was time. He knew he shouldn't, knew he pushed the boundaries if he met with her, but what harm could it do when he'd ensured every avenue had been covered? Six months was a long time to have kept away, and Huntington had admitted he'd relaxed the rigid surveillance on her now. She'd proven she wasn't going to reveal any secrets, he'd said.

Bishop thought back to two weeks after he'd last seen her. How he'd changed into inconspicuous clothing—jeans, white T-shirt, tan leather jacket and a pair of black hiking boots. In his bathroom, he'd applied a thick blond moustache and goatee, a wig, then popped in dark green contacts.

His heart thumping wildly, he slapped a red baseball cap on and left his place, getting into his new, unremarkable, light blue Renault. He drove to the supermarket Fallan worked at, knowing he shouldn't, knowing that area of the city was out of bounds, but failing to see how Huntington could have both him and Fallan watched constantly and justify the expense.

He parked and sat for a good ten minutes staring at the store, imagining her inside. Would she be stacking shelves or working the till? Would she even be in the main shop? She'd told him that last day she sometimes worked in the rear warehouse or up in the offices, wherever she was needed. The thought of coming this far and not seeing her almost made Bishop start the engine and get the fuck back home.

Almost.

He got out of the car and headed to the main store doors, taking a basket from the stack just inside, then covertly glanced at the row of tills, seeing a couple of black-haired workers — none of them Fallan. Like any other customer, he started at one end of the shop with the intent of going down every aisle and picking up a few supplies. He was doing nothing wrong – just grocery shopping, right?

Yeah, you just tell yourself that, man.

He paced the aisles twice just in case he'd missed her the first time. He couldn't imagine he would have – he'd know her anywhere – but she was nowhere in sight. Maybe she was sick. Maybe she didn't work every day. Dejected, but knowing it was probably for the best, he'd bought a bottle of whisky and returned home.

The drink he swigged did nothing to deaden the ache inside him – it never did. About to pour a second, a touch of the devil invaded him. Before he could talk himself out of it, he'd gone to the cupboard under the stairs and taken out a pay-as-you-go mobile. He decided to put a plan into action for down the line, when things got too much and he had to see her, couldn't take being without her a second longer.

In the kitchen, he inserted the battery and SIM, plugged it into the mains and dialled the number of an office-letting company, thumb hovering over the connect call button.

I shouldn't be doing this. Not here. Think it through properly.

He placed the phone on the worktop and went back into the living room while it charged. Three hours passed – hours he'd spent pacing, telling himself making contact with her was insane, could cost them both their lives. The need to hear her overshadowed everything else, though, and he took the phone off charge and went back out in his car again. He parked in a nondescript street on the outskirts of the city then walked – and kept walking – until he was far enough away from his vehicle that if Huntington had a tracker on it he wouldn't connect the phone call with the car's location.

Sitting on a park bench, he called a letting company and arranged to view an office…

He'd met with the realtor, paid a year's rent in advance under the name of David Wilkins, and had gone about setting up a business that for all intents and purposes was a solicitor's. With his know-how, he'd faked transactions and clients. The business thrived without him ever having to set foot in the place or do a speck of work. On paper, it looked to be what he'd intended.

Now, with the burning need to finally put his plan into action, disguised with a prosthetic face, he went inside the building, pulled keys from his pocket and entered the office space he'd rented. Sitting on a chair behind an empty desk, he dialled Fallan's number on the landline. His heart raced, he felt sick and very nearly cut the call. This was wrong, so dangerously wrong, but if he could just hear her…

"Hello?" she said.

He melted at the sound of her beautiful tone. "Miss Jones?" He lowered his voice, adopted a different accent. Scottish. "I'm calling on behalf of Wilkins Solicitors. My name is David Wilkins and I'd like to set up a meeting with you in regards to your late parents."

"Oh. Right. What is this about?"

The pain in her voice made him feel an arsehole, but when she knew why he'd done it she'd understand.

"It's come to light you're due some inheritance, but there are a few details I need from you before I can release the money. Would it be possible to set up a meeting in, say, half an hour?"

"What, *today*?" she asked, sounding incredulous.

"If that's possible, yes."

"Where is your office, and how do I know you're not just some crazy bastard?"

Bishop held back laughter. God, he'd missed her. "You'll find our office in the *Yellow Pages*, if you'd like to check, but we're in Dentham Street. Been in business for five months."

"Um, okay... Half an hour, you say?"

"Yes, if that's at all possible." *Please come. Please...*

"All right." She sounded sceptical, dragging the last word out. "Answer me this. What are my parents' names?"

He gave them.

"And their dates of birth?"

He gave them.

"The places they were born?"

He gave them.

"Okay, Mr Wilkins, was it? I'll see you in half an hour then."

Bishop paced in front of the desk for the whole half an hour. He had the sudden need to visit the toilet — what he was doing was against every rule — but, fuck, he'd waited long enough. He went over everything in his mind. Six months had passed. The solicitor business was a good cover. If Huntington or some other agent had listened to his call to Fallan, they could do some digging and find nothing untoward. Her parents were dead — there was no reason why an inheritance shouldn't be due. No reason why a few visits to this office weren't in order. Bishop hadn't thought beyond that, hadn't made plans for how they could meet after the time when his supposed business of giving her the inheritance was complete. He hoped together they would come up with something that would keep them safe.

The sound of the outer building door opening on squeaking hinges had him jumping and smoothing down his suit. Sweat dampened his palms, and he took a few deep breaths to calm his nerves. What if she'd got over him? What if seeing him again hurt her more than keeping away? What if he'd royally fucked up? He'd have to take it as it came, get a feel during the meeting. He didn't have to tell her right away he was Bishop—his disguise and voice would keep his real identity safe.

A knock sounded on his office door, and he quickly went over to the desk and yanked open a drawer. He took out some papers and scattered them on the desk, then grabbed a laptop and placed it in the centre, lifting the screen and switching it on. As the chime for Windows began, he cleared his throat and walked to the door.

She's here. Jesus fuck, she's here.

He swung open the door.

"Hello, Bishop." Huntington stared at his agent.

Oh, Bishop was good, could very well have pulled this scam off, but one thing had let him down. He'd switched his pay-as-you-go phone on in his residence all those months ago, setting off alarms on Huntington's surveillance equipment. When a call had finally been made on it—even in another location—following the trail had been a breeze. Huntington could only assume Bishop had been blinded by his need to contact Miss Jones again and hadn't realised his mistake. Still, he'd realise it now.

"Uh, I think you have me mixed up with someone else," Bishop said, maintaining his Scottish accent.

"I think not." Huntington pushed past him into the office and sat on the chair behind the desk. He waved impatiently. "Shut the bloody door, man. Great mask, by the way. Did you use government supplies?"

Bishop closed the door, and, instead of the slumped shoulders of defeat Huntington had expected, his agent faced him squarely, remorse absent from his fake face.

"I needed to see her," Bishop said, accent his own. "It wouldn't have done any harm. I waited, gave her enough time to find someone else. Enough time for her to prove she wasn't going to say a fucking word. She hasn't, right? She's kept her end of the bargain."

"Yes, she has. You, however…" Huntington waved again. "Sit. You may need to."

"Why? Easier to have me killed when I'm off my feet, is it? Got men outside ready to do the job once you've left?"

"Oh, stop being such a petulant brat, Bishop. Honestly, you sound like a lovesick fool."

"Good. I am one." Bishop plonked himself in the chair opposite the desk and began removing his mask.

Huntington enjoyed toying with him, would enjoy seeing his face when another agent walked in here soon. Bishop had done exactly what Huntington had predicted — he really did love Miss Jones, and, despite the threat to their lives if Bishop contacted her, the man had done so anyway. Huntington wasn't a complete arsehole. He understood love, knew what it could do to a man, but the government came first and always would. He couldn't allow Bishop to fuck everything up because of his dick, his feelings. When his other agent walked in, everything would fall into place. Or not. If Bishop fucked up again, if he didn't obey the rules he'd be given, he would be terminated.

Bishop winced as he tugged the last of the mask away. His skin looked a little sore where the glue had been, but that was nothing compared with how sore another part of him would be, come tonight. *If* things went to plan.

"So get on with it," Bishop said, his face showing no emotion whatsoever. "I'm busted. I can't do this shit anymore without Fallan in my life. I tried, it sucked, it hurt. So take the pain away, will you? Sooner rather than later." He puffed out his chest as though creating an easier target for a bullet.

Huntington smiled. "You were a fool to think I wouldn't know what you would do. Granted, I didn't think you'd go into such an elaborate set-up, nor did I think you'd wait so long, but I should have known an agent such as you wouldn't do anything by halves. Except you made a little mistake, and, if it wasn't for that, you'd possibly be fucking Miss Jones on this desk right now."

"Fuck!" Bishop rubbed his forehead. "Where is she? What have you done to her?"

Huntington chuckled. "Nothing."

"Oh, Jesus. Don't take this out on her. She didn't know it was me. She thinks I'm a solicitor. Thinks she's coming here to set an inheritance into motion. Don't kill her, Huntington, she doesn't deserve to suffer for something I did. I was stupid, yes, and, however I fucked up, I don't want to know but—"

"Oh, but I'm going to tell you, just so you know. You set up the mobile phone from your home."

"Shit."

"Yes, shit. A shit move, something I expect my agents not to make. However, I can understand how your feelings got in the way back then, and this is precisely why I didn't want you seeing Miss Jones after the Waterman mission. Being with someone outside the company isn't a good idea, Bishop. You knew that, knew what it would entail. You took the job on the understanding you'd have no serious relationships with normal citizens because of the ramifications, the questions that would inevitably be asked by your partner as to your whereabouts, what you did exactly for a living. It would lead to slip-ups. And, although Miss Jones knew what you did, she didn't quite know the *full* extent of it, did she? Yes, she could have been understanding—knowingly living with a killer, knowing her government did things she hadn't thought possible—but she wouldn't have actually known *all* about it to the degree she needed to. *That* is why, six months ago, you couldn't have continued your relationship with her."

Bishop winced, realisation dawning, Huntington suspected. The truth had hit home at last.

"The thought of not seeing her again…" Bishop swallowed. "Just kill me and be done with it. It's better for everyone."

The door behind Bishop opened, and Huntington smiled at the agent. Bishop didn't turn to see who had entered, but twisted his chair so the agent had a clear shot at his back. Bishop closed his eyes, no doubt bringing the vision of Miss Jones to mind, and Huntington felt a pang of sorrow for the man. He nodded at the agent then stood, walking to the door.

"Better for me, Bishop?" the agent asked, tossing something into his lap.

Huntington watched Bishop pick up a crystal key, jump out of the chair and swivel to face him and the agent.

"Fallan?" Bishop croaked.

Huntington smiled. "I'll leave you two to get reacquainted. Miss Jones—or Terri Fields, as she's currently known—has a lot to tell you."

Huntington stepped out into the foyer and closed the door.

Sometimes you had to have a little faith in love. He only hoped placing Bishop and Terri together as an agent team would work. If it didn't…

Well, he'd deal with that later down the line.

Chapter Sixteen

Terri glanced over at Bishop. She had got used to her new name. Fallan Jones was dead and would never be coming back. She'd made a phone call to Huntington that night six months ago and since then she'd undergone intense training to bring her up to the standard of a secret agent.

She'd been taught how to shoot a firearm and look after herself. Been shown the art of disguise and to use the technology they gave her.

"You know, plugging that phone in from home wasn't the brightest idea," she said, "and if you'd done your research you'd have found out Fallan Jones died in a car crash. Seems she drank too much one night and with all the mounting debts she just wanted an out. I still have the same phone number and address, but Terri lives there now." She walked around the office, secretly impressed with the detail he'd put into getting in touch with her.

"Whose idea was that?" Bishop asked.

"Huntington's. He thought you wouldn't be that into checking the local papers. He was right."

"So why do you still have your old number and you're 'dead'? If Fallan doesn't live there but Terri does, neighbours will still see you as you," he said. "Moving to a new location would have been better."

Terri turned and looked at the man she'd changed her entire life for. He appeared so tired, so not himself. Her heart pounded hard. Had she made the right choice in answering his call? God, she knew how much she wanted him, but how would he take the fact that she was an agent? Would it change things between them now she fully understood how dangerous his job was? Now she'd have jobs like that of her own?

"Huntington thought you might get in touch and I was instructed to wait for your call, to live in the house until you made contact. Why did you wait so long?"

"Why did you agree to be Huntington's pet?"

So many questions. Didn't he like the effort she'd put into being with him?

"I'm not his pet," she told him and placed her hands on her hips.

"No? Looked to me like you've become a favoured pet. Huntington, as always, gets what he wants." He sounded so pissed off.

"What is your fucking deal? You left me at that house six months ago. You left me with nothing to keep me going except memories and emotions. I was told you'd be killed if you came after me but they didn't say anything about me coming to you as an agent." She pointed at him. "I couldn't live without you. I love you, Bishop. I didn't set out to fall in love with you but, fuck me, I did. I've never hurt so much in my life as since the last time I saw you."

Terri put her arms by her sides and waited for Bishop to respond.

"You didn't have to go to him," Bishop said. "I was finding a way out. A way we could be together."

"You stupid, stupid, stupid man!" she shouted. With each word, her voice grew louder. No longer happy with the gap between them, she stormed up into his face. "They would have killed you. When are you going to realise you're not invincible? You would be dead right now if it wasn't for me changing the game. As soon as they knew you'd called me someone would have taken you out." She reached inside her pocket and pulled out the letter he'd sent her. "This...this gave me hope with every part of my training. I worked my arse off so I could be with you. If it wasn't for your note I would still be dying inside. You walked away and I couldn't deal with it, so in order for us to be together I did the only thing available to me."

He caught hold of her arms and brought her close.

Terri pulled away. "No. No you're not going to stop me from doing this. You're not—"

With one swift move he picked her up and sat her on top of the desk.

She gasped and helped him rid the desk of all obstacles in their way. The laptop landed on the floor and the papers scattered around them. Bishop opened her legs.

He slammed his lips down on hers and she moaned as she got the first taste in what seemed like forever of the man she loved. She'd been without him for so long she growled and wrapped her arms around his neck, refusing to let him leave her wanting more. He thrust his tongue between her parted lips and she tasted him, meeting his tongue and lips with everything she had to offer.

"Fuck, I want you. I want you so bad," Bishop said.

"Then take me. We've got a couple of weeks. I finished my training the other day and I want to celebrate. You've got me for a hell of a lot longer than a fortnight, though, Bishop."

"Shit. The best news I've heard in months." He tore her jacket from her shoulders, followed by her blouse. "I want you so bad," he repeated, groaning next to her ear.

"I want you as well, Bishop." Terri nibbled his ear and ripped off his suit jacket. She wanted his hard body naked and against her.

"Fuck, I won't last. It's been too long…"

"Do I look like I care? Make me come and I'll forgive you for being so lax in contacting me like that." She took his shirt off and pressed herself to him as he removed her bra.

"You've got such gorgeous tits."

They clawed at each other until she was flat on her back with her trousers on one leg. She panted, needing him to fuck her. Bishop eased away from her long enough to let his own trousers fall down to his ankles. His cock sprang out, long, hard and proud. He coated the head in her juice then pierced her with his throbbing length. She screamed out her pleasure and sunk her nails into the flesh of his arse.

"Fuck, you're so tight and hot."

He grabbed her waist and pulled her further onto his shaft. Lust consumed her with need. His hold on her bordered on the point of pain but Terri wouldn't give up being in his arms.

"Love me, fuck me... Just do me, Bishop," she cried out.

His cock felt so good pushing deep inside her, and she wanted him using her body any way he pleased, bringing both of them to a mindless orgasm as had happened in the past—one where she forgot everything but the man on top of her.

"I love you, Fallan."

He eased out of her cunt then plunged back in. He was so thick, each inch he pushed inside caused her to moan and gasp for more.

"Fuck me." She watched as he withdrew all the way out, his cock wet and slick with her juice. Having him between her thighs felt amazing. Her own dirty film as he rammed inside her.

Terri stopped watching and kissed him. He cupped her neck and brought her closer to kiss her harder. Their fucking increased and the desk moved with each thrust of his hips. She held on and gasped as he stared into her eyes, touching a fingertip to her clit, bringing on her orgasm. His thrusts got harder and faster until his cry rent the air and she felt the hot spill of his seed.

Bishop collapsed on top of her and Terri held him close. Finally, he was in her arms. All of her hard work was worth these precious moments.

"I don't want to pull out," he said.

"Then don't. We've got time to indulge. The rest of our lives." Agreeing to be Huntington's agent bitch had brought about many more possibilities.

"I've missed you," he whispered. He kissed her shoulder then gazed at her face.

"I did this for you," she told him.

"I know that now." He kissed her lips.

A tear fell from her eye as another one gathered.

"Please don't cry, baby. I'm not upset that you want to be with me. I just wish I could give you more and you wouldn't have to live with this agent crap at all." He cupped her cheek and tilted her head back. "I love you so much and this job is high risk. I don't want anything happening to you."

Her heart melted over his concern. He wanted to be with her. Was more concerned about her welfare than anything. She touched his cheek and tried her best to reassure him.

"Would you rather us be apart? You planting fake offices and wasting time, money and resources to find me each time I was warned to move on?"

"I needed to see you," he said. "I couldn't think of any other way."

"And I needed to see you. We both got what we wanted, and, if my safety is such a big issue, protect me. Look after me and never leave me."

Bishop kissed her again and picked her up to carry her across the room to a sofa. "I just want to hold you."

Terri snuggled against him and let herself be held, his scent and presence easing the months of worry in her heart and mind.

"So how's your aim with a firearm?" he asked.

Terri laughed. "When I first shot an airgun in practice I caught a guy walking away in the arse. God, I was so awful I thought Huntington was going to let me go on the first day." Terri began to tell him about her time in training.

"How long did it take to shoot a target properly?"

"Over two months. After the first few weeks, though, Huntington got so pissed off at me shooting people and not targets he got a paintball gun. For ages I was forced to train with that."

186

Bishop laughed and it made her aware of his cock stirring back to life.

"You like being inside me?" she asked.

"I don't want to be anywhere else."

She sat on him and lowered, pushing his half-erect cock inside her.

Terri cried out. "How can you be so close again?" she demanded.

"I've got the woman of my dreams in my arms. I don't want anything else but to be with you. So stop stalling and tell me more about your training."

"I look hot when I fight, even though there are some moves I haven't mastered yet. And I love dressing up in disguises. They're so bloody good."

Bishop stared at her.

"What?" she asked.

"You sound so excited about all of this."

"I'm with you and I want to be excited. Speaking of excited, don't forget Huntington has given us your usual two weeks' grace between projects. How cool is that?"

Terri kissed him and began running her fingers over his arms and waist. She didn't want to talk about her training anymore. She wanted his body and his attention on other things — far more enjoyable things.

"Sweetheart, you're messing with fire," he warned.

"Then burn me." Terri thrust her breasts up against his face and waited for him to nibble on them.

He stared at her for a few seconds before he opened his lips and took a nipple between his teeth. He suckled then pulled away. "You're doing this to shut me up, shoving your tits at me."

"Nope. Just don't want to be swapping work stories when we've got other important matters at hand. Like catching up on six months' worth of sex. I've not had another lover since you."

He frowned at her then gave her a smile that had her pussy contracting. Fuck, he had the cutest smile.

"I've not had anyone else since you, either. I can't believe you kept the letter," he admitted.

"Why? All girls keep love letters."

"Let's get out of here."

"No. I want you to fuck me here on this sofa and then we'll get out of here." She began moving on his lap, his cock hard and firm, her pussy wet from their orgasms.

She was ready for more.

Terri held him while he changed their position. He placed her on her back and made slow, long love to her, loving every inch of her body in the small space. She wrapped her legs around his waist and gave herself over to his capable and expert hands.

As they rested afterwards, the pains of the last few months became insignificant against the immense pleasure to be had in their future. Not only the sex but being in his company. She was so happy. Every time she'd felt down or got hit with depression, she'd thought of this day to get her through. The training was almost brutal at times, and she'd taken out his letter and reread his words. By paying for her house and making sure she had money, Bishop had felt he was taking care of her. It wasn't enough, so she'd contacted Huntington and had stood up against him, looking after their future interests.

She recalled when she'd met Huntington the day after losing Bishop. He'd circled her where she'd stood. Stared at her, hair a mess and her clothes all over the place. He'd taken his gun out of his pocket and pointed it at her head. She'd looked down the barrel and hadn't felt afraid. The shock at her lack of fear had concerned her.

"Do you have any idea the trouble you could be causing?" he'd asked.

"Do I look like I give a fuck?" Fallan had pressed her head harder against the gun.

"You'll be looking down the barrel of a gun one day and someone will shoot you and torture you for information. Do you want to live that life?"

She'd reached up to hold the gun still, making certain it remained there. "Either kill me or fucking train me because I swear to God I'd be more use to you alive than six feet under."

Against all of his better judgements—so he'd said—Huntington had personally trained her. Everything she knew had come from him. Terri had been born...and she would make sure Bishop never ever found out about that incident.

She kissed him on the lips and let him take her to heaven again. The past would remain firmly there and she only needed to worry about a future. With Bishop. How bad could it be?

Epilogue

Bishop, now codename Knight—he'd have to have a word with Huntington about him always choosing chessboard pieces—hunched in the darkness behind a waist-height wall opposite the target building. Terri, going by the name of Ginny for this mission, sat back on her haunches beside him. He couldn't get over how she looked so damn comfortable, as though them launching over the wall in around fifteen minutes would be par for the course. As though storming into the warehouse and possibly killing everyone inside was as boring as working in Asda.

She grinned at him, her smile a flash of light in the gloom, and he smiled back. They'd been working towards this moment for two months, getting along very well as an agent duo, their home life not interfering with work. It was like they had switches in their heads, and, as soon as they returned home, what they did for a living ceased to exist. Just as well. Taking their work home with them didn't really appeal. Knight wanted to spend their spare time getting to know each other better, not talking shop.

They'd both sold their homes, pooling money to buy a trendy top-floor apartment by the Thames. While on downtime they dwelled there as any ordinary couple, only using the hideout flats, houses or cottages when working. They'd revisited the basement a couple of weeks ago, switching off the cameras and having a damn good time, bringing back a thousand memories neither of them had thought they'd ever relive.

It was all in the past now. He wasn't letting her go anywhere without him.

"Two people inside," she said quietly.

"As far as we know." He didn't think there was a possibility of more, but he wanted Ginny on her toes. If she was always on her guard she'd remain safe.

"I bloody doubt there's more," she said. "We've been watching for hours. And I know exactly what you're doing."

"What?" He lifted his night-vision binoculars and gave the warehouse another once-over.

"Making sure I don't get too cocky. No need, Mr Knight. I'm well aware there could be more people inside from before we started today's surveillance." She nudged him in the ribs. "I'm not some china doll who might break."

"You are to me." He moved the binoculars from side to side, seeing nothing but an empty parking lot outside the warehouse and a faint light shining through one of the far-left windows. Then he focused them on her, with her hair pulled back in a low ponytail, a beanie hat jammed low on her brow. Her skin was a mint green colour, giving the impression she was ill.

She sighed. "So seeing me in action, seeing I can shoot someone without batting an eyelid, hasn't convinced you I can take care of myself?" She reached out and covered the lenses with one hand.

He shrugged, aware she might not even have seen it, and lowered the binoculars. "It's not like that. I know you can handle yourself, this job, it's just that... There's a part of me that wants to keep you safe, treat you like a princess. Part of me wishes you weren't even here now. That you were at home, resting on the sofa or taking a long hot bath, waiting for me to come home and fuck you senseless."

"I know, but that's just tough. I am here. I'm not going anywhere. Except into that warehouse with my gun raised and taking out anyone who appears to be a threat."

"They're no threat, just some whackos storing illegal firearms."

"So run that by me again. How can two men with illegal firearms not be a threat?" She laughed quietly, but not unkindly.

He smiled and stared across the deserted road again. "Point taken."

"That's not true."

"What do you mean?" He frowned, wondering what the hell she'd meant. At times she was a puzzle, saying things he didn't understand, for reasons he didn't understand until she decided to make them clear. He'd swear she enjoyed tormenting him, seeing him try to work it out.

"The point hasn't been taken."

"How do you know? If I say the point's been taken, it's been taken. You can't say it hasn't been because you're not me and you don't know how I feel."

"I get what you're saying, but it hasn't been taken, Knight."

He sighed, really not wanting to get into a debate with her right now.

"Not where I want it to be, anyway," she said.

"What the fuck are you talking about, Agent Fields?" He glanced her way, catching another flashing smile. He leaned closer to see her better, just making out a glint in her eye and the suggestion of her trying to hold in laughter.

"Your point, my rear end." She widened her eyes suggestively and licked her lips.

"Ah, I see. *That* point. God, you're a frustrating woman at times. You knew I'd think you meant the other point."

She laughed quietly. "It passes the time, messing about like that."

"So," he said, "you think we've known each other long enough for me to go there now, do you?"

"I think so."

"You only think?"

"All right, I know so."

"Right," he said, holding up a finger to let her know he had information coming through his earpiece.

He nodded twice and peered over the wall, noting a large, dark vehicle hugging the kerb then turning into the parking lot and stopping. Three people emerged — the buyers they'd been waiting for — and he held his breath until the warehouse occupants came outside.

Knight and Ginny observed in silence as a lengthy exchange of money and weapons took place. They seemed to be haggling over the price, and the guns were examined extensively before all five people nodded and shook hands. The buyers climbed back into the car after stowing their purchases in the boot and drove away, followed shortly by another agent's car.

The sellers disappeared back into the building, laughing and joking.

"Ready?" he asked Ginny, his heart beating fast and adrenaline racing through him.

"Yep."

He vaulted over the wall and sped across the road, hearing Ginny's footsteps behind him. They made it to the doors the sellers had gone through, him leaning against the wall on one side, Ginny the other. Damned if he'd ever get used to her doing this job.

Counting to ten, he withdrew his gun and glanced across at his lover.

"In and out, as quickly as we can," he instructed.

Ginny nodded.

"And then, when we get home, Miss Fields, your arse is mine."

About the Author

Natalie Dae

Natalie Dae is a multi-published author in three pen names writing several genres. She lives with her husband, children, and three cats in an English village. She writes full time and is also a cover artist and blog designer. In another life she was an editor. Her other pen names are Sarah Masters and Charley Oweson.

Sam Crescent

Sam Crescent has always had a love of fiction, through her teen years she would find friendship between the pages rather than in an actual person. By the time she turned sixteen she discovered mills and boon and never looked back. She loved the quick happily-ever-after read. A guarantee that no matter what happened the heroes and heroines would always find their soul mate. After college and starting a degree, one lonely bored night she searched the internet looking for a new author to read. On that night and for the years to come she discovered romantica and erotic writing.

Natalie Dae and Sam Crescent love to hear from readers. You can find their contact information, website details and author profile pages at http://www.total-e-bound.com.

Total-E-Bound Publishing

www.total-e-bound.com

Take a look at our exciting range of literagasmic™
erotic romance titles and discover pure quality
at Total-E-Bound.